Dear Jerry,
A good read ♡ W9-BSI-864
Love, Beryl

BOOKS BY GEORGE W. S. TROW

The City in the Mist

Within the Context of No Context

Bullies

THE CITY
IN THE MIST

THE CITY

A NOVEL BY

IN THE MIST

George W. S. Trow

LITTLE, BROWN AND COMPANY   BOSTON   TORONTO

FIRST EDITION

Library of Congress Cataloging in Publication Data

Trow, George W. S.
  The city in the mist.

  I. Title.
PS3570.R647C5   1984   813'.54   83–20911
ISBN 0–316–85307–0

                          VB

              Designed by Dede Cummings

           Published simultaneously in Canada
        by Little, Brown & Company (Canada) Limited

      PRINTED IN THE UNITED STATES OF AMERICA

One

THE CITY IN THE MIST

— 1 —

EDWARD COONLON JONES

MICHAEL COONLON was born in 1845 in New York City. He was descended from a family of criminals and was, all through his young manhood, a criminal himself. A day passed. The sun came up and went down. He spent the day in shebeens and beer gardens and little secret places where you walked down a few stone steps into a dirty, moist cellar where there were all human smells mingled with river damp.

There was bliss in his head. He squeezed a man's neck until the neck was pulp and the man was dead. He did this in the interest of making certain that various taverns, bars, shebeens, and holes-in-the-wall served the brand of beer he represented.

He had great physical strength. He was the strongest of his family. He was one of ten sons of Patrick Coonlon, who was feared but not respected. Patrick Coonlon belonged to the gang of River Rats who pillaged shipping along the North River.

Michael was big, sandy-haired, and strong. He had a great capacity for love. He had an *interest*.

His *interest* was established at the age of six. He was walking with his father when his father said: "Look, Mike, that's Mr. Johannes Aspair. He's the richest man in America."

Michael looked up. He saw a big, lumpish man, obviously not physically strong, walking down a set of steps. He looked up and saw Mr. Aspair's big house. He came back and looked at it again and again.

The house was unusual. It was made out of stone. It was turning black. Already it was very old. Michael Coonlon looked at it and even touched it. It was a continuation of the street. The house looked like a cobblestone street. When it rained (and Michael Coonlon saw it during a rainstorm more than once), water flowed around the stones just as it did in the street.

As a boy, Michael Coonlon looked at the house. As a young man traveling from tavern to tavern in his line of work, he often stopped to look. Leaving one basement dive, headed to another, he would detour to look. In his blissful head there were no contradictions, and it did not seem strange to him to twist a man's arm or squeeze a man's head with the object of promoting the interest of Eagle Beer and then to inspire himself with the view of this house.

His love was for his friend Tom Guin. On the North River docks one day, he saw a man he could not beat with his bare hands. The bliss in his head opened to reveal a thought: this must be my friend.

It was natural that he should try to bring his interest together with his love. One day, in the late afternoon, having spent the day twisting arms and holding heads in a vise grip made from his arm, he took Tom Guin walking. He stopped before the house of Johannes Aspair, the richest man in America. He waved his arm in a simple gesture (as you would in pointing out a champion racehorse) and waited for the meeting of love and interest to occur. It did not occur.

Or at least it did not occur then. Michael Coonlon was downcast by his failure to interest his loved friend in the house, but he did not let go of the friend, and through his friend came a reward: a young woman called Mary Carmody. She was Tom's girl, when Michael met her, and Mike and Tom and Mary went out together: to the Tyrone Gardens (supplied by Eagle Breweries); to the Underwood and the Old Mayfair (likewise supplied); but there came a time when Tom Guin said, "She likes you more than me, Mike," and handed her over.

Shyly, slowly, in a struggle, Michael Coonlon courted Mary Carmody. He had had a wife before; he never gave her a thought: not when they married, not when she gave him sons, not when she died, as she did. But from Mary Carmody his eyes were not averted, and a little more came into them every day.

One night he took her by. He walked with her down the familiar street, feeling the comfort of her, his head leaning down a little, since she was a small woman. His head was hanging down, and his eye was on the pavement, the stones, and on her legs and feet. When they had come to a certain spot he knew, he stopped and turned to her, watched her face and her eyes, as he was learning to do. He had his back to the house.

"He's the richest man in America, Mary," he said.

He watched her. Her face was as round as a circle. Her skin was as fair as daylight. She was smiling.

5

"Oh, Mike, it's the grandest thing I ever saw," she said. And then she began to laugh.

Laughter was not a thing he had expected. He turned around. The house was lit up for a great ball. On the steps of the house there was a woman in costume.

"Look, Mike, she's lit herself up!" Mary Carmody said.

A light blinked on and off, on and off, on top of the woman's head. Mary Carmody laughed. It transformed his life.

MARY CARMODY COONLON died giving birth to a daughter. They were rich by this time. She died in a carved mahogany bed. She had been born in a little shanty in Cork.

"Don't worry, Mike," she said.

Michael Coonlon let out a wail of grief. It was the first sound his daughter heard in life.

The daughter, Sarah, had two half brothers by her father's first, coarse wife. They were eleven and twelve years old at the time of her birth and they did what they could to get their father's attention. They fought and tumbled and bullied one another. Michael Coonlon turned from them.

They were a brewer's family. Everything about them was new. The boys wore new clothes. Michael Coonlon carried money that had just been minted.

Their house was *shiny*. It had been standing for just one year at the time of Sarah Coonlon's birth in 1888. Sarah, fascinated, watched it gleam. One day she stood in the hall perfectly still. She saw that everything was shiny and new. She looked at her own clothes: they were shiny and new. She heard footsteps that she knew to be the footsteps of her father. She waited for him. He found her. He reached into his pocket and gave her a newly minted dollar, which she accepted with cool regard.

They were Irish Catholics living in Albany, New York. They had no social position, although they did have a political one. This meant that the feminine aspect of the family's life was restricted and became unhealthy.

"Here, here, here!" James Coonlon said, pointing to a hole in the wall. John Coonlon brought her over to the hole.

"We'll throw you over if you tell," James said.

She didn't say a word.

They're too old to do things like this, she thought.

She didn't tell. She merely wore her dirty clothes to dinner. She did not wash her face or comb her hair. There were scratches on her arm; red marks. Otherwise, she looked the same as ever: composed and a little severe. She sat down at the dinner table and looked at her soup. Her father looked at her half brothers.

"What's this?" he asked.

"We were playing," said James, sullenly.

"It was an accident," John said.

Their father beat them, and then, not content, he beat them again. There seemed to be no end to his violence.

7

John and James saw possibilities they had not seen before: punishment without end. It seemed to them at moments that they must be near death. They saw a world of violence where men preyed on one another like animals. They saw that they would soon be dead in any world of this kind. They gave up. Their father let them go. They were dirty and ragged. They came out of the library (where they had had their beating) into the hall. Sarah was there, all cleaned up.

Michael Coonlon, Sarah's father, liked to walk around his big house. He walked from room to room. He had two ways of looking at a thing: from the point of view of owning it; from the point of view of working on it. He knew breweries and taverns in this way, but these did not give him so much pleasure as his house. The house was in State Street, opposite the park.

"The house is in the Romanesque style," Sarah said later to her son as they one day entered into the hall.

"Look at the brick!" Michael Coonlon said to the young man on another occasion.

During the building of his house, Michael Coonlon put no distance between himself and the craftsmen who worked on it. He dropped even that small formality he kept up with his brewmasters: he took food with them on the job. This custom led to a free exchange (one that would not have been possible had they, like the brewmasters, continued in his employ), by the terms of which these high craftsmen continued to call at the Coonlon house long after its completion. The doorbell would ring; the maid would come into the parlor or the library.

"It's Sam Koerner, sir, who put in the glass," she would say. Or:

"It's Neilsen, sir, who worked on the floor."

The house was full of light, and colors. Many of the colors were versions of red. Around fireplace openings there were tiles the color of a red fish. Red light lay on the shiny wood floor in geometric figures, advancing and re-treating. The stained-glass windows were brilliant and mostly red.

A source of amazement to Sarah was the front hall. A staircase rose up three stories, all shiny. Colored light was there. As a shiny child, aware of her own cleanness, she would stand in the front hall looking up at the staircase. Later, in the hall, she noticed other things: a small table bearing an empty bowl. She no longer took pleasure in the hall. She passed in and out of it resentfully. *We are not visited*, she thought, thinking of the table and the empty bowl.

Sarah did not like her brothers. When they married, she found that she did not like their wives. When they had sons, she disliked them as well.

She had an aunt, Anna, younger sister of her father. This aunt came to visit Albany when Sarah was ten years old, and for four years afterward Sarah kept her in mind. The aunt was large. She wore voluminous clothes. She lived in Europe. Sarah was impressed.

Sarah took note of her aunt's ways. Her aunt went to church ostentatiously. She used powders and fragrant waters. Small pouches of scented fragments were stuck among her clothes, and when her steamer trunk was

9

opened, heavy smells from Europe rushed out. *This is what it means to be a woman,* Sarah thought.

No one called on the aunt during her visit. Sarah took note. The aunt presented herself as a cosmopolitan about whom it was impossible to predict anything, but Sarah at once predicted that no one would visit her, and no one did.

Sarah stood in the hall to say good-bye to the aunt on the day of her departure for Europe. The aunt went out the door. The steamer trunk went out the door. The door shut behind them, leaving behind some small mingled smells, light, a table, and an empty bowl.

Between the ages of ten and fourteen, Sarah tried to allow herself to be influenced by her idea of her aunt. She bought a bottle of Florida Water and kept it on her bureau. She began to wear a gold cross in a manner she thought of as conspicuous. She tried to dress in clothes in more outward-going colors. But her spirit, which naturally led her to the severe and the pale, rebelled, and she kept alive the idea of her aunt as a Feminine Ideal only by transforming her in her mind (as she had every right to do: time was passing) so that the aunt was reduced in degrees from the voluminous and colorful, until she became, in Sarah's mind, almost thin; almost wistful; almost ironical — almost, in fact, like Sarah herself.

Sarah's aunt lived in Europe, not in any particular country. She spent her life in large hotels; on different verandas; in different dining rooms. She stayed in those countries where it was not unfashionable to be a Roman Catholic.

Sarah's aunt, born Anna Coonlon, was married to a Frenchman called de Herence. She had a daughter, Rita, two years older than Sarah, and a yearly stipend from

Sarah's father. In 1902, when Sarah was fourteen, the aunt returned to Albany with her daughter and Count Herberto de Huerd, an asthmatic Spaniard engaged to the daughter She came with the idea of having her stipend increased to encompass the needs of the de Huerd household soon to be established. Her stipend was increased, but otherwise the visit was not a success.

It was not a success from Sarah's point of view. Her aunt, in actuality, had not grown toward the spiritual and the thin, as the Feminine Ideal had done, but had grown more voluminous and more obviously *coarse*. Sarah resolved, with fierce hatred, to remove traces of her aunt's influence from herself. She decided this and then went to her room immediately, where, looking into a mirror, she discovered that there was very little necessary to do. Her own face was long and thin and pale-skinned, quite unlike her aunt's. She looked into the mirror. Her aunt was utterly irrelevant to what she saw there. What she did see made her a little afraid. Turning away, she began to examine her adornments and her surroundings, not in a spirit of inquiry (which was all done with) but in a businesslike spirit. Her attention fastened on the cross hanging around her neck and on the bottle of Florida Water on her bureau. "Quite harmless," she said aloud. She left them both where they were.

Shortly before the visit was to end, Michael Coonlon took the Spanish asthmatic for a walk. At the age of fifty-seven, Michael Coonlon was a strong man still. It was this fact that he wanted to impress upon the Count. They walked down State Street. They took a streetcar and a ferry to Troy and toured the Coonlon brewery there. Michael Coonlon was attentive. He did not ignore the Count. He instructed him in all the processes of brewing, and intro-

duced him to many of the men who did the work. Together they looked into vats and checked supplies. The
work of fermentation was explained and all the several
smells of a brewery (some of them very pungent) were
introduced into the Count's experience. The Count was
encouraged to taste the product. He was asked if he
could distinguish between Coonlon First and Coonlon
Dark. He was allowed to taste from a batch of Coonlon
Dark that had failed to pass inspection so that he might
know what bad dark beer was. It took most of the day.

They took the streetcar back, but Michael Coonlon,
wanting more exercise, got off with his guest on the out-
skirts of the city. It was a little damp as evening settled in,
but Michael Coonlon did not notice. He was struck by
the beauty of the river and by the way the city of Albany
rose up high above the river. It *was* damp. The Count
began to wheeze. Michael Coonlon walked ahead. He felt
his legs under him. His legs were strong. Several hundreds
of men at a large brewery waited for his look, his word,
any expression of his regard. A noble city rising above a
beautiful river knew his name as a big name. He walked
on. Behind him was a *wheeze*.

They entered the house. The Count tried to catch his
breath but could not. Michael Coonlon looked up. Above
him was the staircase, rising three stories. It never failed
to give him pleasure. Suddenly, he felt an urge to walk
more. He left the house, passing roughly by his guest.

Within the house, the Count collapsed. He could not
catch his breath. A doctor came and said to the Count:
"Certainly you must under no circumstances walk so far
in future."

Rita de Herence said to her mother: "Mama, I think
he knew it would tire Herberto."

Anna Coonlon de Herence looked at the Count. His face was colored in panic. She could see every one of his small teeth.

"I think he thought it would *kill* Herberto," she said.

Dinner that night was for three women: Anna de Herence, her daughter Rita, and her niece Sarah. It was exciting to Sarah to be eating at a table with no men; in general she saw so much of them. Her mood was raised still higher by her secret repudiation of her aunt, who had been adopted secretly, too. Sarah saw herself spinning around the room, now imitating, now rejecting.

Anna de Herence and her daughter talked in solicitous voices about the asthmatic Spaniard who was on an upper story gasping for breath. It occurred to Sarah that she could be rude.

"Father says he's a Count of no account," Sarah said. She allowed herself to use a little brogue in saying this, a thing she had never done before, and which she never in her life did again.

Sarah was lonely and she was proud. She took quick measure and did not retreat from her judgment. She trusted her father, but at times she was uncomfortable even with him. Sometimes when they were walking together, or at night, as he sat by her bed before leaving her (until morning), he would fall into a gentle mood. He would say:

"I didn't have the arm on me *he* had." Or:

"They thought they could put one over on me but they couldn't." Or:

"No one ever put anything over on *her*."

But this made Sarah afraid. Her father saw this, and, with courtesy and kindness, left off. What made her afraid was the gentleness, which found no very strong echo in her; the Irishness, which she did not like; and the sense that she herself was, in some ways, less than her dead mother.

Her mother was not often mentioned, but she was everywhere.

SARAH FOUND A FEMININE IDEAL to replace her aunt, in the person of a young girl of her own age. She saw this young woman from her window. It was a strange thing she felt. It was not that she felt a liking for her or any emotional feeling. Rather, it was: so; what she had felt also at the moment of her birth.

She watched the girl every day for a week. The girl was thin (as she was herself), dark-haired, and was dressed in a school uniform. *As I might be*, Sarah thought. Where Sarah had an ironical look, this girl had utter simplicity. Her severity seemed natural and not, as in Sarah, a challenge. She had an oval face (which became, then, Sarah's ideal) and a great forehead, which was more noticeable for her hair's being pulled back tight against her head.

The girl came always with another girl, also in the uniform. At times they were joined by a young man, a year or two older than they.

Sarah noticed: they did not touch one another or alter their pace. They seemed old. They were not shiny. They did not talk much. A great deal seemed to be already understood.

Once when Sarah was watching, the girl looked up. Sarah fell back from the window as though she had been hit a blow. The next day she did not go to the window, although she longed to go. On the day after that, none of the group of friends appeared in view.

She talked to her father. "These are the people I want to be with," she said. Her father inquired about the uniform and arranged for her to be sent to the school where it was worn. This school was in Troy, on a hill above the town. From the lawn in front of the main building of the school, it was possible to see the Coonlon brewery. *I won't be ashamed of that*, she thought. *It's my father.*

She had no cause to fear. Her severity and her irony kept at a distance those people whose contempt for Irishness was based on the simple idea: they are rowdy. Her reputation for wealth won her other friends. She smiled to think of her vulgar aunt. Another girl, less intelligent, she felt, might have said something about "my aunt who lives in Europe," or "my cousin the Countess de Huerd," but she let it all drop away.

She found that she was welcomed by the girl she had seen from her window. The girl was called Agatha Jones and she lived in Troy. Her cousins the Emerys lived in State Street in Albany. Her family owned the Jones Valve Company. Neither of the girls mentioned the day when their eyes had met. Sometimes, however, Sarah thought that she saw in her friend's eye some secret amusement. She did not take alarm at this, since it was into this style of sardonic pleasure that she herself wanted to enter.

As Sarah's school years drew to a close, it was necessary for her to decide whether or not she would marry Agatha's brother. It presented itself in this way: Should this pleasant

and appropriate rhythm continue or not? If not, it seemed
to Sarah, she would have made no real advance at all.

Both Agatha Jones and her brother, who was named
John Anthony Jones, seemed to be waiting for her to make
a decision. Agatha looked at her sometimes as if to say:
Well?

What decided it, finally, was the Joneses' house in Troy.
It was graceful beyond any house in Sarah's experience.
It was *dull*. It was of limestone. Light entered into it in
such a way that nothing reflected light. Light was somehow absorbed into the air.

One day, John, leaving his sister and mother in a very
pretty upstairs sitting room, took Sarah through all the
house. She knew many of the rooms already, of course:
the large double parlor, the dining room, complete with
portraits of several generations of Joneses (including the
founder of the Valve Company), the small study — all
on the ground floor — and then, upstairs, the sitting room.
But other rooms were new to her: the kitchen, the pantries,
the bedrooms. As she walked through the bedroom where
Mrs. Jones slept, and saw the silver-backed mirror and the
silver-backed comb and the silver-backed brush used by
Mrs. Jones, Sarah thought: Is this a proposal?

"My mother feels that this house is too large for only
herself and Agatha. We would live here," John Jones said.

It was all arranged with great speed, and everything
fell into place as though by an old plan. And as easily as
things changed in that year, which was 1906, so, once
they had changed, they fell away from the idea of change
altogether and Sarah found herself in an atmosphere where
all relationships were fixed. And since nothing much had
been discussed during the time of change, there was no
precedent for discussion afterward. It was settled without

a word that Mrs. Jones and Agatha would leave the house; without a word it was settled that they would visit daily. So that all changes and forces together, whether they were moving or standing still, came to rest near one idea, which was revealed as the generative idea: which had brought her to the hall of her father's house and sent her away from it; which had brought her to her aunt and away from her; which had brought her to her window and back from it. Everything came to rest around the idea that Sarah Jones would receive visits.

Sarah had two children, both girls, in the first years of her marriage. They were called Sally and Fern. Fern grew to be a dull child. Sally, to dullness, added an interest in sports. John Jones professed to like Sally. He ignored Fern. He said that Sally was a *jolly* girl and that Fern was *serious*, although sometimes he said "sober-sided." Sarah took notice of this instance of distinction-making by him, for in general he did not bother with it.

Jolly and Serious were her private names for the girls, and she was at difficulty not to let them be public names as well. Her own judgment of her daughters was: wrong spirit. She liked her house better. The girls were heavy where they should have been light; they were thin where ampleness would have meant strength. The house, on the other hand, had balance. It was four windows wide. There were four window openings on the second floor; on the ground floor the rhythm was: window, *doorway*, window, window.

The house took the weather. The girls did not. In hard weather the girls grew brittle and cracked; in soft weather they *settled*. Seated for too long in an armchair, Sally or Fern began to collect in the cushion. Sarah saw that they

17

would turn into chairs themselves, in time, for some dog or cat or child to sit in. So that this might not happen immediately, she took steps to banish comfort from their lives. She searched the house for upholstery and expelled it. She paused. She opened the door. Air came in from the street. There was a fanlight above, a slender pillar to the left and one to the right. Other furniture — chairs and tables, a sideboard, a desk, other things (but mostly chairs and tables) — came into the house.

She began in the dining room. Here she put the sideboard. At the middle, it curved inward. Some years later, on a tour of the house, Sarah asked her young son Edward Jones: "Why the inward curve, do you suppose?"

Eddy pondered. "A person could stand in the curve," he said.

His mother smiled. Then, very quickly, she kissed his head, which was not a thing she usually did. She said: "My dear Eddy. My dear, dear Eddy." He did not forget the sound of her saying this or the words. He always, ever after, liked *letters* for reason of the salutation: Dear Eddy. My Dear Eddy. Dear. Dear.

Sarah's important work was done in the second-floor sitting room. It was an oval room. There were three door openings. Into one was set a curved door. There was a molding where the ceiling met the walls, and there were broken pediments over each door opening. Otherwise, there was no decoration: no friezes, no panels; but it was, for America, though not large, a very formal room.

The color she wanted was less than ivory; she wanted no evidence of yellow. She ended with a white the color of a healthy child's teeth. When she had this color, she put into the room one dozen Adam-Sheraton painted chairs. Her husband balked at the expense. She went to her father, got the money, and brought to her husband a paper (which he signed) saying that in all circumstances the chairs were hers, paid for by her. It interested her that her husband did not blush or wince or show discomfort as this transaction unfolded. *Just glad not to pay* was her judgment.

She put the chairs into the room and only one thing else: a small painted desk of no particular importance. The chairs were of the greatest beauty. They were a true cream. Their backs were oval, and carried painted decoration: dark green bowknots, light green leaves, red rosebuds. The chairs were put around the room like guests at a party. Some were put against the wall, some stood out in the room. One was put behind the painted desk. Here Sarah sat, at times, like a teacher addressing a class of prize pupils.

As Sarah approached the end of her work in the house, she found that she was again with child. Strangely, given her previous experience with children, she did not resent it. She moved in cool acceptance. When her term was complete, she saw that she had a son. She looked down and thought: a friend.

When the time came to choose a name for the boy, John Anthony Jones, his sister, and his mother went through, once again, the register of family names — Newlen, Albart, Van Griift — which had yielded material to identify the girls. "Coonlon," Sarah said. "Edward *Coonlon* Jones."

⸺⦃ 2 ⦄⸺

THE CITY IN THE MIST

DWARD JONES was raised by his mother. His eyes opened and he saw: his mother. There were noises to hear, but it was the sound of her voice — cool and low and certain — that entered his ear. What he loved was enclosed by that voice; and that voice directed him to what he should look at and what he should love. He was in several circumstances during the time they were together — in his grandfather's big house in Albany, with his big, rough grandfather; in the house in Troy, with his father, among his father's people, with his sisters. But the cool, low voice was constantly his instructor, curving him away from the activities of his father and the approaches of his sisters; bringing him within an understanding of what might be revealed by an angle of light; telling him to spend time alone in a room so that he should know the pleasure of being alone without fear; opening up the definition of fineness so that there was room in it for the roughness of his grandfather, so that he should not be cut off from vigorous love. From the moment Eddy heard the voice of his mother, he was proof against bombast: no shout had power over him. No raised voice had meaning. Authority was for him a cool voice, low and certain; feminine, but with reference to the strength of a man.

⁌

WHEN SALLY REACHED the age of six, in 1914, Sarah, opening her eyes for a moment to the existence of her older daughter, decided to solve the question of her education. It was Sarah's intention to arrive at an answer, impose it decisively, and then, absent a disaster (which she did not mean to occur), to impose it on Fern as well. She consulted a magazine. Sally saw her do it. Sally, six, dull but not stupid, came into the nursery where her mother never came and found her mother with a magazine. Her mother did not ever read magazines. Sally kept still. Her instinct was: keep still. She stood quiet for more than one minute. She had never done this before. She saw her room, her friendly nursery (the province of Nurse Gerdler, herself, and Fern) differently. She saw motes of dust in the light. She saw that a curtain had been torn — a piece of lace hung ragged from one edge. She saw her own bed. She did not like the experience of it.

Her mother looked up. "I've picked a school for you, dear," she said. "Come look."

Sally did not move. Her mother looked at her. A moment passed.

"Very well, let Mummy tell you about it then," Sarah said. "It's called Mount Airy Hall. It is to be found" — and here Sarah paused as she looked more closely at the magazine — "in Journers, New Jersey. It is *small, select;* all classes are conducted in French."

Sally looked at her mother and did not speak.

"Well, then, it's settled," Sarah said. It was settled. Both girls went to Mount Airy Hall for years and years. It was the only education they ever had. Fern taught there for a while before marrying. Sally served on the Board of Directors. Sally occasionally spoke at Assemblies. She always said that her school days were the happiest of her life and that she was grateful for the chance to go to Mount Airy Hall. She was sincere. What she meant was that she was grateful not to have had to attend whatever school it was that met in the upstairs sitting room of her mother's house.

Edward's education was handled differently. He met with his mother from ten in the morning until noon, and again from two in the afternoon until four.

"Here; sit here."

"Yes, Mama."

"Do you know what that stool is?"

"No, Mama."

"It is the work of a man."

He was never shown a tool or a workplace, but object by object he learned the work of the crafts. Work, ever after, had a fascination for him, although he knew only its result. When he saw on the street a man with a tool or saw in a shop a head bent over a task, he would see in his mind the rooms of his mother. *They do it for her,* he thought. He did not ever separate process from result, or step from result into process. He was outside both. The message he had from his mother was: for a reason I cannot tell you, nothing will be required of you. You will be perfect. There is nothing for you to do except sit before the fire. Yet, something may come of it.

His mother never mentioned to any other member of the family any of the things they talked about. Her eyes were open during the hours when they were alone. Later in the afternoon, humor came to her. He could see it. A joke came into her eyes and something else: a glaze over the joke; so that laughter (which was suddenly the subject of her thought) did not pass out of her or into her, but stood still, an object in the middle distance of what she chose to see, which was to a horizon that was formed at a line just above the eyes of other persons.

※

EDDY WAS VERY FAVORED by his grandfather. Once, his grandfather took him to a large political ball. It was called the Policemen's Ball, but it was a political event. It was held in a huge hall, square and dirty. The floor was filled with folding chairs facing a stage. Around the floor was a gallery. He sat with his grandfather in the first seats of the gallery, right over the stage. He felt at perfect ease. There was entertainment. His grandfather roared with laughter. Men and women hit one another on the stage. Eddy looked at their faces and their bodies. They were caked with muddy flesh on their faces. Sweat dripped to the floor of the stage. A man carried a rowboat around his middle. It went on and on. The lights came up. The chairs were pulled away for dancing. Scores of men came forward to greet his grandfather. Each one shook his hand too. He, Eddy, was polite and pleased. His grandfather was pleased. It was a happy night. They left before the dancing.

SOMETIMES WHEN EDDY STAYED with his grandfather, his grandfather would surprise him with a trip. On these occasions his grandfather would appear at his bedroom door early in the morning accompanied by a friend of his called Jerry. Jerry drove. It was a wonderful fact of Michael Coonlon's life that when he needed a thing done, he sent a message to one man or other and that man, pleased to be asked, did what needed to be done.

On a morning, remembered by Edward Jones thereafter, his grandfather appeared at his door with Jerry and announced a trip to New York City.

They drove down the west side of the Hudson River. Eddy sat next to Jerry so he could see the countryside. His grandfather sat in back.

Jerry could not remark too much on the number of fine qualities he found in young Edward Jones. When Eddy pointed out a thing, Jerry praised his eyesight ("I never would have spotted that!"). If Eddy put out an opinion, Jerry, instead of responding with an opinion of his own, would shake his head with great seriousness and say, "Smart as a whip." But most of all what Jerry admired in his friend's grandson was the quality of his turnout and the correctness of his behavior.

"Like a Lord" was Jerry's conclusion.

"The Duke of Albany," Michael Coonlon said.
Eddy was seven years old.

Later, Eddy remembers the day in this way:
They come to a ferry. The car stops. Suddenly they
are among people. He and his grandfather board the ferry;
Jerry stays with the car. He, Eddy, looks and looks.

He sees: fading paint; gold letters; a handrail. He feels:
cold; moisture; a cold handrail; warmth; pricks of wool;
his grandfather. He is covered by: mist.

In the middle of the river there is a mist. The ferry is
suddenly in mist. Eddy stands close to his grandfather at
the rail. He stands so close he can feel his grandfather.

His grandfather says:

> There were two friends.
> Tom Guin. Michael Coonlon.

Eddy puts his hand on the rail. He feels cold moisture.

> Tom Guin. Michael Coonlon.
> Tom and I worked on the docks at that time. We were
> what you call dock wallopers. One day O'Grady, the gang
> boss, slips out to Skelly's to have a beer and he tells me
> to stand in for him. As soon as he's gone, Tom Guin sits
> down. Wasn't going to work, you see. The rest of them
> look at me, what I'm going to do. Oh, he was a big man,
> Eddy. He was the strongest man I ever saw. He could do
> the work of ten men. So he sits there grinning at me — to
> see what I'm going to do. So I took up a shifting bar and
> creased him across the brow with it. We were friends
> after that.
> A day I'll never forget, Eddy. Tom Guin's racket. Peo-

25

THE CITY IN THE MIST

ple talked about it for twenty years. You never saw such
a thing. Three hay barges lashed together. And the food!
And the music! He had two steam propeller boats to pull
it all and two tugs. All up the river. There must have
been ten thousand people. That was politics in those days.

I didn't know there could be so much happiness.

Eddy, your grandmother was Tom Guin's girl at first,
but at the end of the day Tom said, "She likes you better
than me, Mike." And that's the way it was. People wondered we didn't quarrel, but there wasn't a chance of a
quarrel with us.

Real friends don't quarrel, Eddy. They stay friends forever. That's the way it is.

Eddy, as an old man, remembers: quiet, noise from the
water and the ferry. He sees the young boy on the ferry.
On the ferry, the young boy thinks: *how interesting.* His
grandfather says:

I've been lucky.

His grandfather says:

I get the idea: bring it to the old man myself. So, bold
as brass, I go down to Prince Street and knock on his
door. It was a little bit of an office. I said: "Here's the
rent. I'm Michael Coonlon, 323 West Twenty-seventh
Street." I wanted him to know my name, you see. So he
looks up and nods. He takes the money and counts it.
That was Mr. Johannes Aspair, Eddy. He was the richest
man in America.

The richest man in America, young Eddy thinks, *how
interesting.*

The boy looks. Everything is grey. All at once he sees the city of his grandfather's youth. It is the most curious place. He sees palaces there and a man with no nose and a woman dressed up like an electric light. He sees his handsome grandfather. It makes him want to cry out. But he does not cry out.

Oh yes

he thinks.

Show me, please.

It is entirely grey. Suddenly he sees the landing. As an old man he thinks: It is by an act of kindness that a city existed and will exist again. It is by an act of kindness to the ferryman that the ferry slip exists and suddenly appears so that the rush of feet may rush onto firm land instead of circling around angrily.

BY THE YEAR 1931 there had been several changes in the financial situation of Edward Jones's family. The Coonlon brewery had been closed for many years due to Prohibition; Michael Coonlon had not, like others of his competitors, turned to the manufacture of tonic waters and diluted beer; he did not, like his sons, anticipate a reopening. He shut down his business and grew used to the idea of being less rich. The Boys, having suffered a contraction in one part of their inheritance, expanded else-

27

where and were successful in bootlegging. They bullied other people and one another, worked within an atmosphere that was dim and secret, and found for the first time in their lives a congenial occupation.

Eddy's father went bankrupt. Eddy saw him shrink and collapse. John Anthony Jones knew only one rhythm and he knew it in a perfunctory way. In bankruptcy, he suffered from a feeling of clumsiness and entered immediately into the extremity of alcoholism. One day, Sarah opened a drawer and found a bottle of liquor, half full, poorly stopped, liquid seeping from it. Her mind went back to his proposal of marriage. *Must I respond to this?* she wondered.

She said: "Drink if you want to. You needn't hide it from me."

He said: "I don't hide it from *you*." She thought he meant that he hid it from their children.

He did not hide it from them. He took his daughters into his confidence. His daughters, unmarried young women, fluttered about him. They were always, it seemed, in a conference of whispers. Agatha Jones and Mrs. Jones (she was now very old) were in and out of the house.

One day Sarah came into her sitting room, which she kept as a private place for herself and her son, and found her husband writhing on the floor. His arms and legs jerked wildly and fell with force on what was in their way: beautiful chairs — dark green against cream; light green leaves; red rosebuds.

The girls appeared almost at once. Sarah, in this instance, retreated before them. Quickly, a doctor came, and the ancient Mrs. Jones, and Agatha Jones, Sarah's old school friend. This crowd worked with single-minded purpose within Sarah's sitting room without giving any thought to its scheme of decoration. The girls, making clear a space for their sick and anguished father, pushed the chairs into one corner of the room, where they formed no pattern at all. After a time, Agatha Jones, who was more detached than the others in her point of view, pulled one of the chairs out of the corner and sat on it. She sat gracefully, as she always did, but it might have been a packing crate to her. Sarah looked at her friend sitting there. Agatha looked back. Sarah felt *surprise*. In Agatha's look she saw the agony of her husband, which she had not seen before.

The family met together that night. An institution was mentioned as the place where John Anthony Jones must necessarily spend a long stretch of time. Its name was brought into conversation *simply*.

"He knows the place?" Sarah asked.

"Oh, we all know it, I guess," Mrs. Jones said.

Sarah's impulse was to snatch her son and run away.

"Does my son have this?" she asked.

"It passes through *women*, Sarah," Mrs. Jones said. "You will notice that Agatha has not married, although she is a most beautiful and most gifted person, and very deserving to be married."

Sarah looked. Mrs. Jones put her old hand on Agatha's hand. She stroked Agatha's hand as she once had stroked her hair, perhaps, or her brow. This now was the important fact in the room.

Mrs. Jones said: "You do not need to worry about the health of your son, you see, or the health of your daughters either."

The room looked at Sarah. It was a room of mothers and daughters. Mrs. Jones continued to stroke the hand of her daughter. Agatha sat still and allowed it. Fern and Sally sat quietly, longing for the old woman's touch.

"If he had not begun to drink, you would never have known," Mrs. Jones said. She took back her hand to herself.

"We have never liked you, Sarah, but we admire your health," she said.

❇

SARAH LOST HER HEALTH. She took her son and her chairs and her clothes and went back to Albany to live in her father's house.

She retreated. She neglected her son. Her father saw that she had been defeated in her project. He sought to make up any deficit that appeared as a result of her trouble. He looked out for his grandson.

❇

IN THE AUTUMN OF 1932, Sarah Jones died and Michael Coonlon put on his last strength. Deep into old age, he rose early in the morning. He walked his house, talking to dead friends, consulting with himself. After a month, the talks went out-of-doors. It was December; he walked in the snow. He walked about the town, looking into things. He called at the Bank of Commerce & Industry.

Men of business called at the house. His sons, now nearing old age themselves, were called to the house. Then there was a pause. He stayed quiet. The doctor came and went. He rested more. Then, visitors were sent away (the ones who had come before), and another man came. Tall, thin, handsome and bearded, this man wore a black suit, a shirt of the purest white, and a starched standing collar. He conferred with Michael Coonlon. At first, Michael Coonlon came down to the study to receive him. Later, the man went upstairs to see him in the room where he was. One day, Edward was summoned to this room.

It was his grandparents' bedroom. High in a tower on the third floor, it looked out on the park. There were wide windows, and above each one, smaller windows inset with leaded stained glass. The bed was carved mahogany. There was a fireplace framed in red tiles.

His grandfather was in bed. The man in the black suit stood at his grandfather's right hand. Eddy approached his grandfather and stood by his left hand. His grandfather gave him both his hands, which were of undiminished strength — strong and good. His grandfather said:

"This is the gentleman we were speaking of, Robert. Master Edward Jones. Eddy, shake the hand of Mr. Prain." Edward moved around the bed and put out his hand to the man in the black suit, who took it in a friendly way.

"I am pleased to meet you, sir," Edward said.

"And how many years have *you?*" the man in the black suit said, as though he were about to reveal how many he had himself.

"Twelve, sir. Thirteen on March fourteenth."

His grandfather spoke. He said:

"Eddy, I have one thing to tell you. Mr. Prain is the most respected man in Albany. If he says it, it goes. Do you understand me?"

Edward said: "Yes, sir."

"If you should have a problem, you go knock on his

door. I don't say a word about your father, who has troubles of his own, or a word about your uncles, who have troubles of their own, or a word about anyone. All I say is: Here is Mr. Robert Prain. If you have a problem, knock on his door."

The three men were silent. Eddy was afraid that he would cry, but he did not cry. Mr. Prain then said: "Do you know where my door is, Eddy?"

Edward said: "Oh yes, sir. Everyone knows where you live."

Michael Coonlon got up from his bed in mid-February, 1933. Eddy spent his days with him. Tutors came to the house. It was agreed that while Michael Coonlon lived, Eddy would not go to school in a regular way. *This is more important* was the message he had from his grandfather at this time.

Michael Coonlon measured his energy. He knew how much he had and what it would do. He built up his strength, although he knew it would leave him soon after it had been built up. Sometimes he was in strength for one hour; sometimes for twenty minutes. All the time he had in strength was used to find protection for his grandson. He looked. He thought. *Protection that will last,* he thought. Michael Coonlon talked to the living and to the dead. He looked into each piece of property he had and judged where the strength was in it, and the weakness.

Eddy was alone for many hours each day. He would be alone in a room and then his grandfather would appear. Eddy was not startled when his grandfather entered a room or when he left: no time was wasted feigning surprise or anxiety. Eddy listened. His grandfather spoke in long stories, often, but sometimes they enclosed a small sentence that was like a length of wire. His grandfather said:

"The Boys think they take after me. They are right. You take after *her*."

"The Boys want the brewery. Let them have it. You keep the real estate."

"Trust *property*."

"Don't complain; the world is good."

"When there's commotion, you stay still."

"Take inventory."

Michael Coonlon went back to his bed, but the talks continued. Sometimes Michael Coonlon rambled, but Eddy was not alarmed. The maids and the nurse let him see things they would have pulled another child away from.

Michael Coonlon drifted back past his daughter to the time of his wife, but he kept hold of Eddy while he drifted. Sometimes he held Eddy's hand tight, as though that would keep the order right. He told Eddy things Eddy could hardly understand, but he understood them.

The Dead Rabbits had a jump-up. Me and Oddy the Jew got into it over did they kill Toomy McDonald. They said they did; that was good enough for us, and we jumped on them. Two of us, six of them. Wasn't Oddy the one! He could rip your arm off, Eddy, just pull it. He pulled three men off me.

We got the Albert Gardens so they wouldn't take beer except from us. So I go in one day and look behind the bar and I taste it, and I spit it out. This isn't Eagle, I say, and I just look and he spills: they're putting Hammer's stuff in our kegs, charging the Eagle price for that swill. So I walk calm as you please and open every keg. Taste it. "What's Eagle stays; what's Hammer gets poured on the floor," I say. They did it, too. You should have seen them, Eddy, pouring their own cheap beer bought and paid for on their own floor. They did it. They couldn't say no to me by then. When they were done, Eddy, they put up a sign: CLOSED FOR RENOVATION. I had to laugh at that.

Tom Guin was the strongest, Eddy. The only one I couldn't beat with my bare fists.

Eddy sat still. He knew certain things to ask. Sometimes when his grandfather drifted, it was into sleep; Eddy just sat beside him, glad to see him taking rest. Sometimes the drifting was a trouble: he saw his grandfather reach for a thing and not get to it. Then he knew to ask one question or another to bring back a favorite story. After a time, the only stories that would bring him back to strength were stories about Mary Carmody.

Oh, she was a one. You couldn't put one over on her. And smart! You take after her, Eddy.

Good books are good friends, Eddy. That's what she said. She'd want you to keep right on, get your education.

Eddy, I was the darkest fool when I met her. You know what I was, a roughneck. That's a kind word for it. What did I know: squeeze the other fellow. I'd be doing it still. Where would I be? In this handsome house? No. No. I looked at her, Eddy. She wasn't five foot two. I looked at her and I looked at her. I don't know what to say. I just looked at her. Always be gentle with a woman, Eddy.

The Boys came more often. They came with their wives and their own boys, who were puffy and red. Together in

34

a room they talked easily. When Eddy came in they shut up. Their talk to one another was of the brewery and the coming importance of the brewery. Of the brewery and the Boys, Michael Coonlon said: "They'll be out of business in six months."

By late spring he was dying. Eddy felt himself suddenly in fear. The death of the old man loomed. He felt what he would need and not have. He wanted to crawl into the bed of the old man and die with him. He cried. The old man saw him cry. The old man said:

Do not be afraid.
My hand will protect you.
And money.
And *her*. Mary Carmody, you never knew, looks after you.

He lifted himself up. He sat up. He moved forward as if to grab at something. He said:

What she did!

He said it again, loud.

What she did!

It was the only shout Eddy ever heard. It fixed him in place. It ran through him. The old Irish voice, strong as bells. The old Irish man, strong as an old tree, shouted out to his dead wife:

Mary, help the boy!

35

"What she did," he said, low, telling the most powerful thing he knew,

> took me up from ruffian, from thug, from killer, Eddy, from killer. Took me up in her arms, accepted me, made me a man, made me gentle. What she said: "Who are you, ruffian?" A small man, however big I was.
> I couldn't stand the pain of it. She looked. She looked at me. "What do you want, a brewery?" she asked.
> I stood still, Eddy. I stood still. I said, "Yes, Mary. A brewery."
> "Save your money," she said. "We'll have a brewery."

The old man looked at him, his eyes wide, the enormity of the idea come to him again. Eddy was crying. The old man let moments of silence pass so that the sound of the boy crying could be heard.

Eddy *heaved*. He gasped for breath.

"Come close," the old man said. "Let me tell you a story."

Michael Coonlon was as light as air. The story was simple and sweet. His grandson lay beside him in bed, his head on his chest. He told him a story that was story after story: how money was saved; a house bought; money put away; property bought.

> And she says to me one day: "Mike, we're going to Albany." And by then I don't question her. We sell what we have and it comes to something. I never had anything before. Before, I had what I had in my pocket. Now I've got something. What does a pocket matter?
> And she says to me one day: "Mike, we're ready, get the ticket." And I go and I get the ticket. And I think:

save money. I learn her lesson, save money, and I get two seats and I come back and she says, "Show me the ticket." So I show it to her and she laughs and she says, "You're a regular Scotchman" — pleased, you see, because I could never save a dime — and then she says: "Go back and get us a *room.*" And I say: "A room, Mary, a drawing room?" And I go back and I get a drawing room. Oh, Eddy, it was grand! Big plush seats, nice red, you ring a bell the man comes! What a trip, Eddy! Along the river. It was lovely. It was the Erie Shandaken. That was the rich man's road. It was a rich man's trip. And I have been a rich man ever since.

Eddy lay with the old man through the night. The nurse came and watched over them both. It was not something that could be disturbed. In the grey light, Eddy awoke and went to his room. During the light of day, he did not go to see his grandfather. He roamed the house, seeing every room but the tower where his grandfather was. A voice told him: Take inventory.

He understood that his grandfather would die soon. He went to his own room and organized his own clothes, taking note of what was ready to be worn.

The house filled up. The Boys, their wives, their boys, a priest, the doctor. At six o'clock the door was opened to Mr. Prain. The Boys gave way, pressed forward, both. Mr. Prain was shown to the tower. After a time he came to Eddy's room. He said:

Your grandfather is still alive, but he is very ill. It is distressing to see him. I think he is of two minds as to whether to send for you or not. Shortly, you and I will have to begin to make decisions together. Perhaps we should make this decision together.

37

Eddy went with Mr. Prain to the tower. Mr. Prain opened the door but did not enter. When Eddy went in, the nurse left. Eddy saw that it was important not to cry or to notice the terrible look on his grandfather's face, the growing presence of death. His grandfather reached out in pleasure: "Eddy," he said. Eddy went to his grandfather. His grandfather spoke to him, spending all his breath. Beside him in his bed he had a little packet, wrapped up in old cloth. "Take it," he said to Eddy. Eddy picked it up. He knew he was meant to open it and he did. Inside was a small bottle of whiskey and a button, a small button of mother-of-pearl. The button had no holes for thread. It was of a size not suitable for most buttonholes. It was hard to tell if it belonged to something pertaining to a man, or something meant for a woman.

"That's what I had when I met her," Michael Coonlon said. He took his breath in rapidly. "All I had." Michael Coonlon sent to every part, looking for whatever strength had been overlooked. "I was in with the Pearl Button Gang," he said. "I was a thug." His eyes moved. His eyes moved over years. He saw death and murder; men choking on liquor, gagging on blood. His eyes moved over the button. "No one will ever lay a hand on you," he said.

Michael Coonlon was laid out. The casket was fully open. The Boys, asked "What clothes?" by Mr. Boynton of Boynton & Ross, looked at one another in confusion. Eddy said: his morning suit; grey waistcoat; grey four-in-hand tie. He showed Mr. Boynton's assistant, Mr. Fairwether, where to find these clothes. Mr. Fairwether followed him up the stairs to the tower. Eddy opened the double doors to his grandfather's closet. He and Mr. Fairwether saw all his grandfather's clothes spread out: his grandfather's hats, nicely brushed; his shoes, nicely shined; all his good clothes. Eddy looked. These clothes belonged to him, Eddy. He took inventory. All the things in the house were his, and the house, and other property too. He spent that summer with Mr. and Mrs. Robert Prain at their camp in the Adirondacks. In the fall he went away to school. The house was divided into apartments. He kept the third floor for himself. He stayed in it for one week each year. His other real property (given him by his grandfather) included two houses on Lark Street, a warehouse down the hill, and the land under Goldblatt's, Kerney & Stewart's, Junlan's, and Freer's stores. He had, for the rest of his life, in good times and bad, good income from these holdings. He had securities too, and he managed these with skill, so that the shape of his holdings was different from year to year; but he did not alter the arrangement of real estate he had been given. It was like an old garden, something best left to itself. At first the land under the stores produced the most income; when the stores declined, the houses suddenly rose in value. When the decline of the stores was complete and the rise in value of the houses was complete, the warehouse was condemned and yielded several hundred thousand dollars. The Coonlon brewery did go broke, and the Boys, who had done so well as bootleggers, came to curse Repeal.

Mr. Boynton, tactful man, learned how to proceed. He looked at the Boys respectfully, asked the question, and sent his ear out to catch the answer from Eddy. *In the library*, Eddy said.

For two days, Eddy sat with his grandfather, who was dead. It was not difficult for him to do it. He knew the room. He knew what to do. He watched over the book and saw that it was signed. Flowers came. Flowers filled the house. No flower was turned away or sent to a hospital. Florence Coonlon, wife of James, older of the Boys, made a beginning of taking charge. "Oh, there're *too many*," she said, busying herself with work she did not understand.

"No, not too many," Eddy said. He arranged them. The house filled up. Four fire companies from Albany, three from Troy, companies from Cohoes and Watervliet — all these sent arrangements of flowers: roses arranged on wire — horseshoes, stars, circles. The Young Men's Hibernian Club sent a harp eight feet tall made of carnations dyed green.

"Oh no!" Florence Coonlon said, learning to strive away from the Young Hibernians, keeping her own son out of it. "What do we do with *that*?"

"Put it in the stairwell," Eddy said.

Politicians came: the Mayor of Troy and all the aldermen; the Mayor of Albany and the aldermen of Albany. The Governor came.

Brewers and ex-brewers came: Mr. Polinsky of Heroedler's; old Mr. Bulton of Bulton's, with his son; Jack Sweeney and Roscoe Flynn of Handel's, with their wives and children. These were brewery owners who had been successful men and hoped to be so again, although Mr. Polinsky wondered if it would ever be the same.

Brewery workers came: German-Americans and Irish-Americans and men of New England stock. They brought their wives and sons. Eddy stood. He was a young man, with a slight body and a big head. He was not solemn, but he was serious-looking. He was wearing a fine black suit, a starched white shirt, and a black four-in-hand tie. He stood. Beside him was a low table with a book to sign.

A person had to bend down to sign it. Rising up again a person would see: Eddy; his fine turnout; and his dark, adult eyes.

The Boys came and went from the room. They were loud in greeting this one or that one (or they were suddenly struck sad and mournful), but they were not steady.

Eddy stood at his post throughout two days. He begrudged the small time he spent away. He regarded each person who came as someone of the greatest importance, since each person was connected to his grandfather. He saw that some people came only out of curiosity, but it reflected well on his grandfather that people were interested in him, he thought; others were merely doing a duty, but that was a part of it too, he thought. His *political* instinct told him to shake every hand, and he did. Some people who had come out of curiosity or out of duty were surprised to find, when they were back on the street, that the memory of a big Irishman laid out and the feel of the small hand of his grandson stayed in mind.

Eddy was rewarded many times. True mourners came and each one of these stopped to tell him a word. One man gave Eddy a silver dollar. He said:

I worked for him and my father worked for him and he was the best man I ever knew. I tell you the first time I saw him. I was walking with my father, and down the street he comes, tall and handsome, as you know, dressed like a gentleman as he is today. And my father says: "Do you know who that is? That's Michael Coonlon." And I say, "Oh, Father, do you know him?" And my father says, "Indeed." And then, of a sudden, I take fright. I think, What if he don't know us? And I fear for my father. But then, of a sudden, it's all right. He comes up and takes my father by the hand and don't let go and talks like the one thing missing in the day was to see my father. Oh, I was proud. And then he says, looking at me: "You bring your boy to me when he's ready to work," and it's settled. He reaches in his pocket and gives me a silver dollar to close the deal. I thought to myself, a boy's thought, that I'd give it back if he ever needed help, which he never did, thank God. But maybe you could use it now, having lost such a friend; so here you are, keep it.

Eddy said, "Thank you," and put it in his pocket.

The German workmen came: Helmut Neilsen, who worked in wood, and Sam Koerner, who worked in glass and lead. Eddy saw their names as they wrote them in the book. They were old men, and shy. They had come from far away. Eddy said: "Please stay with us in the house." He saw to it that they were taken care of. He said: "Will you please follow the casket at the funeral." He knew that they would worry about their dress. "Mr. Boynton will have the right clothes for you," he said.

Policemen in shifts of eight stood guard at the door of the house in dress uniform. They kept the line right. The Modern Woodsmen came and the Odd Fellows and the Elks and the Moose. The Odd Fellows sent white daisies and red carnations; the Modern Woodsmen, bronze and yellow mums; the Elks sent roses; the Moose sent carnations. The Modern Woodsmen also sent a tree: a tree of wire — trunk of roses, limbs of gladiolas.

The hours of visitation ended at nine o'clock each night. There was no food or drink. *No liquor*, Eddy thought. He knew what he could do and what he could not do. He could not arrange a wake or control it. The Boys went along, wanting to play down expense; their wives agreed, wanting to play down Irishness. The Boys brought flasks for themselves, though.

At the end of the second day of visitation, Eddy stood with his grandfather for a moment and then he went up to his room. Take inventory, he told himself. In his room there was an arrangement of pink daisies and a vase of red gladiolas and yellow mums. He read the cards: "Father Dennis Hallohan"; "Mr. and Mrs. Travery." I wish I knew who you were, Eddy thought. He thought: almost good enough.

He left his room. He walked down the staircase. There were flowers on each step. There were flowers in wicker baskets and in baskets of ceramic material; there were flowers in vases of every shape.

He reached the hall. He looked up. The staircase rose up flight after flight. There were flowers on each step. The hall was filled. The tree of roses and gladiolas rose up high. The harp from the Young Hibernians rose up. He saw diamonds of roses, circles of roses and carnations, angles of daisies and mums and carnations and gladiolas and snapdragons. Almost good enough, he thought.

He walked across the grass. He was alone. He thought: *lonely*; but he did not feel it. He stood still; a small wind blew past. He saw himself in room after room. In a library, waiting for his grandfather. In a sitting room, waiting for his mother. In rooms he did not know and had yet to visit. He was not uncomfortable.

He approached a handsome house. He knocked on the door. A servant, an old man, answered. "I am Edward Jones," Eddy told the servant.

He walked through the house. He looked. He saw

43

Chinese things; things he did not know. He wanted badly to stop and look closely. He felt the high ceiling. How *high,* he thought.

He entered a large library. There were shelves from the floor to the high ceiling, filled with books. Many books were bound in leather and the titles of many books were stamped in gold. Mr. Robert Prain rose and greeted him.

Eddy approached Mr. Prain. He asked in the most polite way if Mr. Prain would be able to come to Michael Coonlon's funeral. Mr. Prain looked for a moment. In the most gentle way, his look said: What's here? He said: "Oh yes, Eddy. I will be there."

"And *Mrs.* Prain. Will Mrs. Prain be able to come?"

"I think Mrs. Prain will be able to come. Yes."

"And your brother, Mr. Prain; Mr. Howard Prain. Will *he* be able to come?"

There was a pause. The two men were silent and watchful.

"I have not spoken to my brother, but I will speak to him if it is important."

"Oh yes; it is important," Eddy said.

Mr. Prain watched. Eddy was still before him. *What? More?* Robert Prain thought. *Go ahead, then,* he thought, a little impatient, wondering, what *is* here?

"Mr. Prain, could you show me the *Chinese things?*" Eddy asked.

The funeral was high mass. The large church was filled. The coffin was escorted by twenty pallbearers. Five fire companies were in uniform, splendid. The church was filled with flowers. Flowers had been brought from the house. They were banked around the altar. *Not too many for here,* Eddy thought. The Jones family came, as was

44

proper. Two hundred policemen came in uniform, splendid. The Mayor of Albany; the Mayor of Troy; the aldermen of both cities; the Moose; the Elks; the Odd Fellows; the Hibernians; the Modern Woodsmen; the Governor and his wife — all came. Mr. Robert C. Prain came in with Mrs. Prain, who had been born a Miss Hope of Hope Hall in Otsego County. Mr. Howard Prain came in with *his* wife, the former Louise Van Horne Van Rensselaer, and her sister, Miss Alida Van Horne Van Rensselaer, and *their* friend Miss Dana from New York City. Mr. Robert Prain brought his son, Mr. Robert Prain, Jr., who was at Harvard, and his daughter Miss Lila Prain, who was still in the schoolroom. Mr. and Mrs. Howard Prain brought their son Edward Mallory Prain, who was eight years old. Edward Jones saw it all. He said to his grandfather: *They all came, Grandaddy.* To himself he thought: Miss Lila Prain; how pretty *she* is.

The picture of this young girl entered his head and stayed with him. It entered his mind, where his dead grandfather was and many other old people besides. There were thugs in his mind and a woman dressed like an electric light. The richest man in America was there in his office in Prince Street. Looking at Miss Lila Prain, Eddy thought: how pretty *she* is.

⸻⸰⊰ 3 ⊱⸰⸻

JOHANNES AND HIS BROTHER

THERE is a city in the mist. Always, when there is a mist, it is possible to imagine a city in it. In this case, the city exists.

There is a ferry, and a ferryman. There is a man on an iron bed, pillows propped up behind him. Both the ferryman and the man in the iron bed see a city that does not exist. The man in bed looks through a grey window and sees the city of his youth. The ferryman, although he is blinded by fog, sees the outline of the landing. His alert ears hear the rush of feet onto the landing; all this while he is blinded by fog, far from shore.

These men are happy.

In his room, the man looking through the grey window thinks about the city of his youth: how the streets were full of people and promised fulfillment of every ambition.

Of every ambition I had then

he thinks. He thinks about various ambitions: to own a pair of reddish-tan shoes; to spend a day at the beach; to own a fine straw hat called a Montecristo; to have pocket money to give to children; to be admired by children.

He grows old. He requires less and less. He is unvisited. His struggle is: not to be overwhelmed by abundance. He takes tiny bites of food. He takes small sips of coffee and liquor. He is drunk at times, but he takes only a small amount of liquor.

He knows the paths of the old city. He watches the old markings. For long periods he stays near home, but sometimes he strikes out on one of the old paths and goes far north into the newly built city. He keeps to the old paths, which lie hidden and unrecognized within the new streets.

He moves with others of his kind. These are men who have an idea of what it is to be noble. They live in places whose names reflect this idea: Hotel Rex; Hotel Prince. These men believe in the existence of a King, although they do not mention him. It is inconceivable to them that there should not be existing somewhere in the city a man of great power who will lift them up.

It is a Nobility. The men in it come to resemble one another. They grow to be so much alike that when one dies, what dies in particular is almost nothing, an infinitesimal thing. These men do not die in their own clothes, for instance. They die in a shirt belonging to another man; in trousers belonging to another man; in shoes belonging to another man. Their shoes are always brown and dry and scuffed; they are in a good style.

Each one has an iron bed. Each one can, at certain moments, feel the shape of the city within which he wanted: everything. At the moment of death, everything is given: a pair of reddish-tan shoes; a day at the beach; a

47

fine straw hat (a Montecristo); pocket money. God descends and gives them these things, and, as a mark of special favor, He causes to hover over the city the shape of the city within which they were wanted.

These old men live until they are at least one hundred years old. At the moment of the death of one of them, there hovers over the city the shape of a much older city. Certain shapes appear again and again. Other forms through which the city has passed are never seen. Any shape that is not held in the mind of at least one man is completely dead and unable to appear since these shapes are a gift for the use of men.

A city seen by many old men, dying, encloses a figure passing down Prince Street toward a small house of two stories and a gable. This is Johannes Aspair II, of that rich family. The city forms itself around him. In his hands are: maps, contracts, covenants, deeds, and mortgages. He owns a place to live in and a place to work in, and the Ninth Ward, and the land around the reservoir, and the land under a store selling silk, and a hotel where thieves live. This is just a sampling of what he owns.

He is heavy. Each fold in his forehead is heavy, like an outcropping of rock; his nose is like granite, and his eyes hang down like lead balls on their way to the ground, halfway along a long fall. He does not smile too much. When he smiles it is at some *silly* thought. When he smiles he is likely, then, to laugh. He laughs at: monkeys dressed up; midgets; the broadest humor.

He is the father of two sons. He has no sisters. His only brother is a half-wit.

Come back to the moment of his birth. A thin, sharp man wearing a high-collared coat and a neckcloth stands over a bed. This man, Johannes Aspair I, bends over his wife and sees a heavy child. At his side is a child fantastically light and thin. Color comes into the father's sharp face as he sees himself *in half*. He looks at his two sons. *It was too much to hold together*, he thinks. *I have come apart*.

The heavy son has much to suffer from his father. He enters into the business at a very early age and bends his head over the details of the work with the devotion of an old man, hoping to please his father, but he looks up from the ledger-book to see his father displeased. *From what cause?* he wonders at first, until he comes to see that the question itself has its origins in a failure of imagination.

Sometimes the heavy son puts his forehead to his brother's forehead, which runs wild with imagination. His brother holds perfectly still for this operation. He is thin, the older brother, and dressed in fine linen. He has a special chair and a special window to sit beside. Later, an enormous house is built for him to live in.

One day, the heavy brother puts his forehead to the forehead of his older brother and holds it there for a long time. His hands grab hold of the older brother. When he takes his head away it occurs to him to look into his brother's face. He sees tears and a glimmer of intelligence.

The heavy brother wins over his father by displaying qualities of resignation and patience. After any failure, he takes up his ledger-books again immediately, to demonstrate that he will not grow bitter over his faults or put aside work on account of a bitter thought.

He does all his father's work for year after year. His father grows old and light. The father in the end weighs less than any detail that comes under the notice of his son. At last he dies. Johannes II buries him and puts him away, detail by detail.

　　　　　　　　　　　⁂

By the time the first Johannes died, Johannes II was old himself. His habits were set. He arose in the old house his father had built in Broadway (surrounded now by commercial enterprises; these, too, growing older and less fashionable) and, shortly thereafter, walked to the Aspair office in Prince Street. There he spent the day, bowed over a ledger-book. Here anyone could seek him out, although few did. An old schoolmate; a young boy bringing rent money; an anthologist — these came by. To the old schoolmate he said, after a time, "What can I do for you?" thinking in his mind of a sum of money, only to find the man rising embarrassedly. He counted out the boy's rent money and entered it into a book. To the anthologist, compiler of a list of "Wealthy Men of the Metropolis," he said: "Would you attend to all this for your room and board?" — which words followed him to his grave and beyond, for they seemed very typical of the rich men of that generation.

The generation changed. Johannes II lived on, and the famous phrase did too, but *room and board* came to mean something different. Fortunes had grown too large to exist only in ledger-books, or too immodest, and the possessors of fortunes gave up the attempt to keep them hidden there. Men lived in marble palaces and contemplated a new dictum, contained in the response of a railroad magnate to a question put to him by a reporter. The response was: "The law, the law, what do I care about the law? Ain't I got the power?" Men contemplated the change in attitude among rich men. Some men noted that the *anthologist* had given way to the *reporter*.

Johannes continued as before, walking from the old house in Broadway to his office in Prince Street, acknowledging no change; but he must have been startled now and again, as he entered the details of his business into his ledger-books, to see how out of all proportion the figures were that presented themselves to be written down. For without his making an effort (beyond the usual attention to detail), and certainly without any exercise of imagination, his fortune had grown to double and then treble what it had been at his father's death, when very many men had wondered if (absent the *light touch* of his father) it would thrive at all.

He did not change, but his sons were of the new generation and they were pulled this way and that. Johannes made no effort to help them; that is, important moments opened up and closed without his saying a word. He made no sign to them that he expected them to follow in his old way; nor did he carry himself in any way that implied the *example*. "I will be doing this, this way, until I die" was what he would have said, had he said anything at all, which he did not. It was said for him, less politely, by a *reporter*, who seemed to find in his old habits a tinge of *hypocrisy* when compared with the overt display of the newer magnates: "He will die as he has lived — his back sloped over a dry and dusty ledger-book, without ever having had, so far as a human being can tell, a moment's real pleasure out of the vast fortune he has extracted from the people of this city."

What were the sons to do? They *writhed*. In the habits of their father, in his house, in his office, in his unconcern for what he lacked and his patient overseeing of what he did have, they saw the imprint of bourgeois Europe; but if they turned away from him, thinking, well, we are Americans, after all, and must find a new way, they came face-to-face with the manners, newly imported, of *princely* Europe (or at least the food and clothes and architecture; the manners were embryonic); nowhere were they offered a role that was Rich and American, both. Their spiritual brothers were, perhaps, in Russia, where some men found that they must leave home for London or Paris if they were not to seem eccentric.

Except that there was no need to leave. London and Paris and other parts of Europe had come to New York. In the milieu rising up around the sons of Johannes Aspair II, there were artifacts from Loire châteaux and imitations of the châteaux themselves; there were Flemish tapestries and Italian refectory tables and Jacobean leaded glass. Men and women were at home in all time and no time. While Johannes Aspair II worked to build a wall of habit around his unruly fortune, the style elsewhere was to give into unruliness. Men and women divvied up all the recent centuries and all the important countries too.

It was a madness, and it obscured, or very nearly obscured, all republican manners. Most especially it obscured the debate about what manners in a republic should be. It was a revolution in a way, and had the momentum of a revolution. It put an end to talk by providing a surfeit of action. But it did more than that. It took the premises of the old debate and twisted them, leaving them so changed that it was nearly impossible afterward to restore them to their earlier condition. For instance, as to the simple distinction between the *gentleman* and the *mob*: a Federalist man of property would have known how to proceed in an argument on this subject, and a Jacksonian Democrat too. But the sons of Johannes II did not know what position to take or even where the old positions were to be found. A rich Federalist might regard with horror the storming of the White House by a mob (which did happen at Jackson's inauguration), but at least he knew what he was seeing. But what were the sons of Johannes Aspair II to make of the equally unmannered mob before them, who were not storming palaces but constructing them?

The revolution of money killed the old debate and cast doubt on its ever having had any importance. In retrospect, it seemed that there had been no debate at all, merely a dance step. The mob had not existed; at least not as a force for democracy. There had been no violation intended, only a kind of party — a precursor of those more luxurious parties of the era under discussion. A man of the age of the sons of Johannes II might have looked back and seen that what the *mob* opposed in the idea of the *gentleman* was not too much privilege, but too little; the mob wanted to oust the gentleman because the gentleman stood in the way of everybody's being a duke.

In the age of the money revolution in which the sons of Johannes II reached maturity, no modest manners had meaning, except that *theirs* did. This was the striking fact to which the attention of James-James and Heinrich Aspair (the sons of Johannes II) was drawn every day. Men who lived in marble palaces uptown altered their route to catch a look at the dirty stone house fronting on Broadway. Some came by every day.

The house was three stories tall. It occupied the northerly half of the city block bounded by Broadway and Mercer Street, Broome Street and Spring Street. The southerly half (also owned by the family, together with the next block and the next and the next, down to Canal Street) was occupied by another old-fashioned stone house, which was no longer maintained as a private residence, and (back of this house; entered from Mercer Street) a livery stable. Next to the livery stable was the stable belonging to the Aspair house. Between the stable and the house was a flagstone courtyard (enclosed by a high wall) in which stood one old oak tree.

It was an old-fashioned house. The people within were old-fashioned people. But there was something about them that defined the modern and aroused the interest of all citizens. It was their fortune: their money. It defined modernity. It was on the modern scale. It established the scale, so to speak; so that each marble house was measured against this old stone one.

The Aspair fortune was created new every day. It was as much a wonder as the oceans and the great plains. The receipts of a day made a fortune; the receipts of a week made a large fortune. In a year were created a company of new millionaires who did not appear in public to build on Fifth Avenue and entertain, but stayed on with Johannes II in the little office in Prince Street, and walked home with him in the grey evening to Broadway.

A regiment of Aspair millionaires kept the old man company. They did not talk to another person. In the morning they followed him to work. Obedient, they stood quietly around his desk. They might have, any one of them, gone around the world on a steam yacht, for example, but they did not. Compact, dense, and strong, they stood around their maker. Or was he merely their *chronicler?* In any case, they came into existence when he made note of their existence in his ledger-book.

They walked home with him at evening. The streets were dim and not entirely clean. *The neighborhood is declining,* one of the newest-made millionaires would say. The older ones, who knew the neighborhood from long ago, didn't say a thing.

They stood around the table at dinner wishing him good appetite. They stood about his bed while he slept. Some of the older ones curled up in a spot at his feet. From time to time he took them to see his brother, who was the only other person they cared for. Johannes II no longer pressed his forehead to his brother's. Instead, he sat quietly with him, hour after hour, while all the millions watched.

Johannes ignored his sons. He rose earlier and earlier. He got up in the black of night. He went through his dark house. How did he care for his person? Did he eat food?

He was alone. He walked in darkness through the streets. He saw forms. He saw the old stone in the street. When it rained, he saw water flow black as ink around the stones. He watched water flow from gutter spouts into the street. Was this the beginning of imagination?

His wife was old; he was older. His sons were in middle age. What was to be done?

His sons waited. Never were sons more eager for the advice of a father. They rose early and dressed. When they heard their father rise, they made a noise. In case he should want to speak . . .

The house had stood past its time. Thieves moved into the adjacent house and wondered that they should be so close. Old men, derelict, touched the old house for luck. The house suited thieves and derelicts. It was dirty and black, they dared to approach it, dirty and black themselves. It was reckoned a gift by them: in general, what they had to touch was failure. But *here* . . . They come close. Stone. Black stone. They look within: all the money in America. Curious!

He summoned his sons. To Heinrich, the younger, he said: "Collect books." To James-James II (namesake of the simple brother), he said: "Marry."

Johannes Aspair II grew to be a creature of imagination. He was in the imagination of every person; every mark entered his head as meaning. He looked at the marks he made with his pen. He saw stones making up the street: stone; stone; stone.

Often he went to see his brother. His brother was dressed like a perfect gentleman. He lived in a beautiful house. He *babbled*. Johannes sat. How he loved his brother. He listened. He could understand something of what his brother was saying.

Heinrich bought books and built a house to keep them in. James-James II married. He chose a southern woman, or allowed himself to be chosen by her. He was exceedingly shy. He inwardly pleaded that someone should notice that he was ready to marry. Later on, his wife, who was called Ama Stone, said to a member of the press:

I brought the Aspairs into Society.

She did bring them into Society. Entering the black stone house she found: an old woman; an old man; a shy man of middle age, her husband. No one resisted her. She saw that she must not under any circumstance tell a lie to any member of the family; otherwise she could do as she pleased. She told them exactly what she was going to do. The old woman, who had never been consulted in anything, merely opened her eyes. The shy man (her husband) looked at his father. There was a moment. The old man thought: perhaps my brother would enjoy it.

Johannes Aspair II said aloud: "Perhaps my brother would enjoy it."

Ama Aspair said: "We will give it in *honor* of your brother."

She made a party for a child. All colors were bright. All lights were dazzling points of light like stars. There was dancing arranged for. And costumes: the most brilliant; the most extreme — all to please a child.

Elsewhere she was ruthless. She let the press in on it and encouraged speculation about who would be asked. "It's an old house," she said. "There isn't much room." She meant to establish a point for all time.

So then, her party had two aspects: a childlike and a ruthless one. There was no contradiction. It was a country of wondrous cruel children, all in costume, looking for joy.

It was an achievement. It made a point for all time. Those who responded to ruthlessness found it; those who were capable of joy saw it. The ruthless were amazed to be in the neighborhood of joy; the joyous saw a reconciliation with the brutal.

Johannes Aspair II sat with his brother in a small sitting room adjoining the big front parlor, which had been

cleared for dancing. He sat in perfect happiness. *Why
have I denied myself this for so long?* he wondered. His
brother babbled cheerfully. Sometimes Johannes could
understand what he said; sometimes not. Ama Aspair
brought guests forward to be introduced to the two old
men. James-James Aspair I looked at each one closely.
Sometimes he reached out to touch a costume or a person,
but only the most handsome person or the most gorgeous
costume.

One by one, Ama Aspair passed each of her guests forward to the old men. When the last guest had passed out
of the little sitting room, she closed the double doors,
shutting them all out. She felt a rush of power. This was
the center of American life, she felt: herself alone with
these two old men, everyone else shut out. She looked at
Johannes Aspair and his brother. She wanted *everything*
from them, but had sense enough not to ask for anything.
Instead she gave something. She went up close to James-
James Aspair and put her face right in front of his. "I want
you to be the first to see," she said. Then she lit herself up.
She had an electric light on her forehead. She blinked on
and off. James-James Aspair was in rapture. He clapped his
hands and opened his eyes wide. In his eyes, Ama Stone
Aspair (Mrs. James-James Aspair II) saw: all success.

The party went on. Kings and queens danced with chil-
dren all night. Young women and men formed a Star
Quadrille, and a Hobby Horse Quadrille, and other figures.
James-James Aspair II saw a little of his shyness disappear.
"I know my father is pleased that you have paid so much
attention to my uncle," he said to his wife.

"Your uncle has taught me a great deal about enter-
taining," she answered.

In the sitting room, James-James Aspair took up his

brother's hand. *Lightness* passed from him to his brother. What an excess of light he had about him. It flowed out of him into his heavy brother. Johannes Aspair, astonished, felt himself rise into a great level plain full of light, and, especially, *color*. Full of gratitude, he struggled to make a return, a bit of his own weight. James-James felt this. In a moment, he spoke (for a moment) with perfect clarity.

"I am one hundred years old," he said.

And then:

"I am dressed like an angel."

THE FAMILY was like a body, at moments; like a flesh man. At other moments it was a house; for a time it seemed to be in ledger-books.

The ledger-books were burned, and then the house. One morning, in his ninety-fifth year, Johannes called a relative of Ama Stone who served as his companion and nurse and told him to bring to the flagstone courtyard between the house and the stable all the ledger-books there were in the Prince Street office, except the most current. The young man, a gentle southerner, was sure the old man intended to destroy them, and delayed. A day passed and another. On the morning of the third day, the old man appeared in his room. "Where are they?" he asked. The young man, afraid, went immediately to the office and supervised the removal of all the Aspair papers (except those that were current) to the courtyard behind the old house in Broadway. There, the old man sat. Cartons were opened and papers passed to him. He judged them quickly

59

Some few were saved; all the others went to feed the high fire in front of him. The old man sat so close to the fire that to approach him was to risk extreme heat. Sometimes it seemed that the papers in his hand must catch on fire. Johannes felt the heat as comfort. He went quickly through the papers. All were familiar; most were in his own hand. He sent nearly everything into the fire. It was hard to find a pattern in what was withheld. But there was a pattern. Any book that contained a reference to the affairs of his brother was set aside and saved — so that while all the ordinary works of the house of Aspair were put into the fire, there remained a complete record of the financial affairs of the one member of the family who never took into his hand so much as one coin. What descended into public knowledge about the work of assembling the Aspair fortune — in the West, in the China trade, in New York City — survived because it was neighbor to this other story, which was the story, told in figures, of the ways in which Johannes looked after his older brother.

Shortly thereafter, the family abandoned the house, and the house burned. Old men watched from their windows at the hotel next door. The other old house on the lots in the square block was now a hotel with a sign: HOTEL SUN. Derelict men watched silently as the house burned. The heat of the fire within the house cracked the mortar between the stones.

What remained was the flesh body of the family. This body the founder saw cut in half: into light and heavy parts. Subsequent divisions broke the body into so many pieces that it was no longer possible to conceive of it as a whole. One man got a smile, or a few old lots, or he inherited a shadowy need to walk alone in the early morning. The men suffered most. To live as James-James or Johannes or Petrus or Corneil or Heinrich or Sixte Aspair was to live in doubt. Each man had his sliver yet was required to act as though he were whole, or *a* whole; while, all the time, the whole slipped away. A man who has had a limb cut off sometimes feels the echo of the limb, or a love for it, or the outline of what it had been; these men — no more, themselves, than a finger of the body — failed to imagine the thing they were missing, turned away from the necessity of attempting it, and tried to find happiness in the attention of those people who did not or could not see how fragmentary they were. Their wives were more at ease: to be *Mrs. Aspair* was the same thing as having a job.

A brief chronicle of the generations after Johannes II would include these facts:

Ama Stone Aspair outlived her husband and, in the last years of her life, removed herself to Europe, where she lived simply in a house adjoining a lemon orchard. Here she wrote a series of naive "letters of instruction" to her daughter-in-law Gladys Aspair (the wife of James-James Aspair III), which she no doubt meant to be published. Gladys Aspair, an ironical woman, did not admire the letters or follow the advice offered in them.

The children of James-James Aspair III and Gladys Aspair were all very handsome. The distinction of this branch of the family grew during the time of the fifth generation in the same way that the fortune of the family as a whole had grown in the days of Johannes II. These Aspairs sat on their name and it grew and grew. Just as Johannes II had watched as the gyrations of other men increased the value of his real estate, so did the Aspairs of the fifth generation see the importance and *publicity value* of their name grow as a result of other people's striving for

61

position. If only these Aspairs had been richer, they would have been happy.

There was money in one branch. The brother of James-James III, another Johannes, noted in himself a certain frugality, a natural weight. He had no instinct for commerce, but he saw that by *not hurting* his money or standing in its way, he might be rich. He married a girl his mother pointed out to him — a small, frugal princess of Parme — and it turned out that she had the same point of view: hold your breath. They were neither happy nor otherwise, except that it made this Johannes a little sad, sometimes, that his mother (to whom he was devoted) found him so dull and that she wrote no "letters of instruction" to his wife.

For one short period, the family fell together again. The young son of Johannes III, yet another Johannes, drowned. He was aboard an ocean liner when it sank. His body was recovered, an incarnation of the family: bloated, changed, corrupted by grossness, but with smooth patches, and, for all its corruption, a compelling beauty. All the family came to look over him.

But it could not last, destiny being otherwise. They parted again. The James-James Aspairs went back to their distinction; the Heinrich Aspairs went back to their civic duties; the Johannes Aspairs returned to their money and to their remaining son, Sixte, who, although still a boy, was already a little heavy, and a little dull. Each Aspair to his sliver. There was a sixth generation and then a seventh. In this generation there was a young woman called Victoria Feldman, granddaughter of Petrus Aspair (a distinguished and handsome man), who was the son of James-James Aspair III (and Gladys Anthus Aspair), who was the son of James-James Aspair II (and Ama Stone Aspair), who was the son of Johannes Aspair II, who was the son of Johannes, the founder. *Her* sliver was a part of Manhattan Island (share of a share of income deriving from neglected lots downtown: rent from a dry-goods concern, the Hotel Rex, the Hotel Prince) — although in another way, all of New York belonged to her, since she was the only Aspair of her generation to attempt to live there.

— *Two* —

MISS QUALITY

—◀{ 4 }▶—

VICTORIA FELDMAN

A MAN passed her and she noticed the heaviness of his lip and the deadness under his eyes though he was a young man. She saw a woman hurrying along as though she had a purpose, but she was sure the woman had none. She felt the heaviness of the city, the way it pressed down on persons, making them feign lightness or speed.

She was tall, with a long, graceful neck. She expected many things to be offered to her and then she would choose one.

She carried a bolt of cloth. A man brushed by her and she was taken by a fear that he was involved in a maneuver with one or two others to get the bolt of cloth from her. Four times in a month someone had come into her apartment and stolen from her, until she had no real jewelry left. Each time, the person coming in had taken her television set and her telephone-answering machine, but these she replaced.

She was alone on a two-dimensioned plane. She felt like

a stick intruding upon an otherwise unbroken surface. The buildings around her had flattened out; they all lay comfortably on the plane, which ran up to her feet and rushed away beyond her, pausing for her, leaving her unflattened but alone.

She returned to her house. She paused outside. She noticed its crumbling brownstone, the gross balusters, the thick handrail, all crumbling. She went up to the front door. She entered into the hallway and then went up a flight of stairs. There was a smell, but she was used to it.

Once in her home, she set down the bolt of cloth and went to her telephone-answering machine. She touched it, and into the room came the voice of an angry person:

> This is Emily Dicter. It is ten o'clock. You were supposed to be here at nine-thirty with the fabric. I can get someone else, you know.

You will get someone else, Victoria thought. *You won't have me.* She looked at her room. She had propped the bolt of cloth against the side of the fireplace. She would have to move it, but perhaps she would not. Often, she ended up leaving a thing where she had put it first. Look. Look at her room. It is planted around with specimens like the bolt of cloth. It is by no means ugly.

Her gift with rooms came from her father. He worried. He saw a chair, for example, and it worried him if the slats were wrong. One way or another, he set them right. Out of necessity, he learned many crafts. He could build a boat, for instance.

He *pushed things together*. He pushed pieces of wood into each other. He pushed a chair up to a table and pushed

68

them, together, against a wall. He lived in a shed and pushed it next to a store, and then pushed the two, together, into a small house, and this was where he lived.

If I don't work anymore, Victoria thought to herself, *I won't have any money, but I might get some somewhere.*

Suddenly, she began to be fearful, not because she was worried about money, but because her thought was the sort of thought her father had: that he would get some somewhere.

She thought of things she had heard said about her father:

> He was like a man from the bazaar. You know, if your ship stops at a port where there is a good bazaar, a man comes aboard who is dressed in clothes of a very good cut and you wonder who he could be and it turns out that he is an agent for tailors in the bazaar. He was like that.

> He made us all laugh.

> He was not a fortune hunter. In fact, he had a lot of money, I think. I think he thought it would have more *chic* if he acted poor since he was a Jew.

> He cultivated the gypsy. Actually he was very shrewd. He gave me very good advice about my real estate.

She got into her bed, which was a carved Italian sofa, almost simple, upon which there lay a horsehair mattress that could be covered during the day. She lay on her back, looking up at the high ceiling. Her feet were cramped at the bottom of the bed, so she hung her left leg out over the edge. She never had a bed big enough. She felt her hair cushion her head. She had wonderful hair. It was abundant and each strand was thick. It was curly or straight, whichever she wanted it to be.

She drifted into sleep. She could see through her thin eyelids up to the ceiling of the room. *Clean*, she thought. *Clean*.

She was awakened many hours later by a telephone call. She felt that she did not want to hear her own voice on the telephone-answering machine, so she picked up the receiver. It was her mother. Her mother said:

> Post, the great pig, hasn't sent the check for this month. I called the office and a voice out of Brooklyn says, "I'm sorry, Mrs. Post, Mr. Post is on his boat and we don't have the authorization." *Authorization*, don't you love it?

The conversation ended after a time and Victoria went back into her bed, but her peace had been destroyed by her mother. Trying to dream of her father, she was visited by her mother. She had a very few shreds of her father; her mother was everywhere around. On a rare occasion she would meet someone who remembered her father and she would inquire about him and strain her bad memory to remember everything that was said. For news of her mother she did not have to move one step. There was a small, snaggletoothed woman — a grotesque creature, with a hanging, wet upper lip and just one hat, red, which she wore at all times — who knocked on Victoria's door in a kind of a frenzy on those occasions (more and more infrequent) when her mother's name was mentioned in the "Nina Knows" column of the morning tabloid. These visits were, perhaps, the ugliest feature of her life, in Victoria's opinion, and caused her to suffer headaches and from a malaise, which showed itself in a reluctance to eat or leave the apartment.

She felt a malaise coming on now and she fought against it. She had qualities of bravery and fortitude, and had it been necessary for her to do something valiant to save her country, she could have done it. For herself she was able to do less, but she put up an effort.

When the man she was seeing called, she said she would go out.

The man she was seeing would often call at the last minute. Often he would ask her to come to a restaurant to meet him; when she got there she would find that he was finishing a meal with a business associate or someone he was trying to impress.

Or sometimes, she dined with this man and, after a time, he got restless and went to telephone someone else to come and join them.

This time she found her friend with two other men. One was of medium height, with a round face and thin, reddish hair; he was the sort of Irishman who is not impractical and "priest-ridden," but shrewd and contemptuous of all people. The other was thick and short. He seemed to have been rented somehow for the occasion.

No one spoke to her, although the thick man acknowledged her coming by moving his chair to one side to give her more space. It was a very crowded restaurant.

Then suddenly her friend turned to her and gave a summary of the talk he had been having with the reddish Irishman. He did this quickly, with a kind of perfunctory energy. He was "filling in" an associate or dictating a letter to a secretary or telling a story quickly because there was no time; no time.

He took over the company two years ago. Profits continued to increase, but unit sales were down. They brought in Mr. Kull, whom you've heard of, ummm, maybe not, but, last year we talked to the Relay Group? Also involved in that, *considerable* success. But here no. He moved too quickly, discounting, for instance, to compete with the discounters, but his own customers, rural women, had no access to discounters, so he destroyed his profit margin for no reason. The worst case, you see. Old-fashioned management; the base slowly eroding; then *quick fix*; quick trip to a better base, but before that is established the old one takes fright, or flight, leaving a period in which only the most enormous capital investment will help bridge the gap, which was not available . . . hence . . .

He waved his arm. The thick man made no move. The Irish man nodded and nodded.

A waiter brought a tray of desserts. Victoria smiled at him and shook her head. She was hungry, but she was afraid that her malaise would appear in the form of disgust if she touched food; and, in any case, how could she begin with dessert? Her friend waved the waiter away without looking at him. Then a curious thing happened: the reddish man selected two desserts, took them from the tray himself, and set them in front of the thick man. The thick man tasted from both of the sweets. His face showed no expression. The reddish man looked at him closely.

The people with whom her friend took meals in restaurants were likely to be strange. Once, she had had a meal with a woman whose son, a cripple, was holding ten people hostage in a subway car, during the time of the dinner and on through that night. She had met many political men whose careers had ended, in disgrace or not, and other people who could only be described as curiosities: mad people who had crazy theories about the world. These, especially, seemed to fascinate her friend, an Englishman, who regarded them as essentially American.

With these people, Victoria felt very uncomfortable — as though she were a kind of traitor; she did not know much about the history of herself or of the city she lived in or of her country, but she had a feeling that it was not a good thing to regard craziness as the force of creation. She was uncomfortable now in this restaurant with her friend and these two men and she wondered if they were crazy or not. Then she thought: no; he's tasting the food to make sure there's no poison in it. But this did not make her more calm.

She felt herself to be in the center of a great vacuum that would open itself like a great jaw. She was not afraid, but she did not feel any longer like a social creature and this made her apprehensive. But this apprehension was a weak thing, generated out of the warmth, the actual temperature of the proximity of people, and it receded as she found the proximity to be producing only coolness. The people and objects around her were suppressed, leaving her alone on a flat landscape where the only sensations were of herself and a little warm breeze.

All this vanished and she found herself in the restaurant again. Quickly, she rose and went to her friend and made as though to kiss him. In the end she could not do it, but she was able to kiss her own hand and then put her hand on him (although she did not offer the part of the hand she had kissed); and she tried to put into this gesture a sense that *so many things are understood between us,* but she thought immediately that she might have failed in this.

On the street she felt the force of the city full in her

73

face. She felt it as a great wind blowing against her, slow-
ing her progress. All at once she felt all the solidness of
things and her own more tender nature. Buildings were of
stone. Streets were of stone. She understood the necessity
of people's futile attempt at some light quality.

Feldman was my fling

her mother sometimes said, in the face of pain; separation;
failure. Or she said:

I was the first girl in my set to marry a Jew.

Victoria tried to remember her father, but words, dates,
facts, and the present all belonged to her mother. She
walked. She came out of the solid street into one that was
mostly color and light. She found a newsstand and looked
at what was offered. She bought a copy of the early edition
of the morning tabloid. She opened to the "Nina Knows"
column, but she didn't have the heart for it. She glanced
over the afternoon tabloid.

TERROR TOT SCREAMS IN RAGE

was the headline. She shuddered to think of a tot screaming in rage. Still, there was something about it. Compelling.
She wondered would she be asked to go to a restaurant and
there would be a small child: the terror tot. *I won't be able
to do that anymore*, she thought. *One more thing.*
She walked on. She hurried back to the solid street, but
found it empty. The line of buildings receded on each side.
It opened up like a long prospect in a garden where one

74

was not welcome. Soon people who were at home there would come out and stare. The thought drove her on.

I was at home here

she thought.

But not now.

She thought: *What will I do about him?* — meaning the man she was seeing. *Well, we can go to parties anyway.* He was different out of restaurants: kinder to her, more like a gentleman. In people's houses he didn't care so much for curiosities. He looked after his placement at dinner. He cultivated all the women around him and asked each one to write him a book. He was the head of a publishing firm.

She returned to her house. On the stairs she was taken by a fear that she would meet someone and have to talk, but she passed into her apartment without meeting a soul. The bolt of cloth stood against the side of the fireplace. Other things were in their places. She got into her bed and soon felt that she was in *her* place.

She awoke within two hours. She was surrounded by unease. Unease *caulked* her. She was almost shut. Her eyes were gently glued, and her lips. She freed herself.

She returned to the streets. It was not possible to stay at home. The streets were full of people. She sought the places where the street was most full. Her ordinary care was gone. She looked disheveled and she felt that people were looking at her strangely.

She returned to the newsstand. The streets were emptying. She put down a coin and took a copy of the afternoon tabloid.

She was fascinated by a feature called "Miss Quality." Miss Quality was a young woman, younger than herself, who went to all the parties around town and wrote them up. Victoria was interested because she never recognized any of the people mentioned in "Miss Quality," and yet there was something familiar about everything in the column.

Miss Quality went to large, ugly discotheques; she went with the police to raid after-hours clubs; she knew children who lived in condemned buildings. Her heroes were certain *humorists*, and what she praised as "quality" was merely a willingness, in obscure or vicious people, to sacrifice what little substance they were possessed of to the nourishment of a "personal style" that was destined to die quickly. And yet her *point of view* was familiar.

> Feldman was my fling.
> I was the first girl in my set to marry a Jew.

It was like that: the jauntiness of someone enormously rich who had decided to go everywhere, do everything, and the devil may care. Victoria knew how her mother had come by this point of view: her mother's idea was that she was rebelling against certain *old dowagers*. What the woman in the newspaper thought she was doing, Victoria could not guess. There was a photograph of Miss Quality: a rather plump girl in a tight riding jacket, curly hair, smoking a cigarette. Victoria found her to be rather sweet-looking.

Miss Quality also wrote news stories about violent crime.

TERROR TOT SCREAMS IN RAGE

It disturbed her. Nevertheless, she read on. The child's mother belonged to what the newspaper called a Terror Cult. The child had been inducted into it. The Terror Cult had ordered the mother to kill her paramour, who had threatened to go to the police. The child had watched as . . .

Victoria put the paper down. She put it down in the street. She laid it gently, like a small corpse. She felt its deadness. It was quiet. She considered the different kinds of quiet: the quiet night; the quiet grasses; the quiet city.

THE SUN CAME UP. Light shone on the fireplace and the bolt of cloth, on chairs, tables, and rugs. Victoria opened her eyes gratefully. Her eyes opened; her mouth opened; she stretched herself, moving her left leg out of the bed. Playfully, she shook her leg, admiring its form at the same time, and then she laughed.

Sometimes when the night had been very bad, the morning was particularly fresh for her. At these times she worked happily in her rooms, and sometimes she took out a book and read it, or took out a book of blank pages in which she kept reminiscences of her father.

Daddy could set up a room in twenty-five minutes

the first entry in this book ran.

Most of what was written was brief, and there were many things blotted out and changed. Her handwriting began as a big scrawl, but became smaller. The paper had a good weight.

The longest and most substantial entry was this:

I met my father for the first time when I was twelve years old. My mother and I and Frank Post were on Frank Post's boat and I heard my mother say, "My God, it's Feldman." We were anchored in a little sound in the region of the Ten Thousand Islands. A small boat, only a dinghy, was coming towards us. In it was a man with a dark face and a big straw hat.

Frank Post invited my father aboard and we had lunch. Frank Post always had good food and my father appreciated that. There was chilled wine and a good fresh chicken salad. My father expressed no surprise to find us. Neither did my mother or Frank Post express any surprise after my mother said, "My God, it's Feldman." They did not inquire after anything or anybody. Conversation was about the food and the weather, how the fishing had been and what had been caught.

I didn't say anything. No one had said anything about this man's being my father. He didn't seem to notice me much, or to look my way. I looked at him sometimes, but more often I looked at my mother, who seemed much calmer than usual.

It was very calm in the little sound. You could hear every small thing. We all sat together as though we were all old friends who had been traveling a long time together, happily.

At the end of lunch my father, in a very businesslike way, said, "I don't know your plan, but if you are coming back to the islands, you might come to me for lunch when you do. In the meantime Victoria could stay with me."

For two weeks I stayed with him. Elsewhere I have tried to put down what I remember about the way his house looked and what he told me about how he put it together. If I could express what he told me correctly, it would be a book, but so far I have been unable to do that. To summarize, I would say that I was very quiet the whole time, and he was very patient.

I do not mean that he was quiet. My father was in a kind of frenzy during the time I was with him. He would stay up all night. Sometimes I could hear a little *scraping* noise; sometimes I heard nothing. But when I came downstairs in the morning, the house would be filled with new things. He was *teaching me*. Since I left him I have tried to make use of what he taught me. Sometimes it slips away from me. Perhaps if I use it wrongly it will be taken away by force.

Victoria read over this entry and thought of adding to it, but did not. She asked herself if her gift was gone for good now. In a moment she looked over to where the bolt of cloth lay against the fireplace. Cloth coming loose from the roll hung in beautiful folds.

She stayed in that day, but went out during the afternoon of the next, and almost immediately she saw a man she knew but did not like. *Don't snub him,* she thought.

She did not snub him. She went to a chocolate shop with him and let him buy her a package of dark chocolates in the shape of seashells. She went with him to a flower shop and advised him on which cut flowers to buy. Here, not absentminded, she left the chocolates. The man, who was called Simon Green, did not remark on it. Outside the flower shop, she turned to him quickly; looked right at him.

79

His face was like a small melon. Around his nose and under his eyes were blood vessels bursting to the surface. "Do you know what we should do?" Victoria said — as though to an old friend, at the end of the day, putting one more thing into the afternoon before parting — "we should go to Fragattzi's Gallery. I have a feeling they will be terribly pretty."

Simon Green followed. She came to Fragattzi's Gallery. She went immediately to one drawing as though to say: everything begins here; and she began to move from one drawing to the next. Immediately, she began to forget Simon Green. The drawings, which were architectural renderings in the *Beaux Arts* style, took her eyes. She followed lines. She followed spaces between ranks of columns. *Palaces*, she thought. She looked up. From across the room a small man bowed to her — actually bowed. Victoria nodded and smiled. *Who can he be?* she asked herself. Kind man. Wish I were with him.

Victoria Feldman let Simon Green walk her home. *Don't snub him*, she thought. She didn't, but she put on an abstracted air. He left her. He was thinking: *maybe*. At parting, her foot on the step, she remembered who the small man was who had bowed to her at Fragattzi's Gallery; or she almost remembered. *Friend of Lila Codman's*, she thought. She turned. Simon Green was walking off. He showed her the back of his head, the small melon head. She wanted to shout: "Oh, that man? He's an old friend of my cousin Lila Codman. I forget his name." It was too late. It was a lost opportunity.

Inside the front door, the conversation continued.

VICTORIA FELDMAN: Oh, I remember now. It's Eddy Jones.

SIMON GREEN [*very impressed*]: Is Lila Codman your cousin? I didn't know that.

VICTORIA FELDMAN [*confident*]: Oh, well, she was married to my mother's cousin Sixte Aspair, you know.

⸱⸰⸰{ 5 }⸰⸰⸱

MISS QUALITY

HALF awake, Miss Quality perceived murders.

MOM STUFFS TOT IN DRYER

HERO COP GUNNED BY PORNO KING

QUEER TWINS IN ODD DEATH DUO

The bedclothes were rumpled. She moved a lot in sleep. The comforter was on the floor. She slept with it in all weathers. For a while. Satin stuff, it slithered off onto the floor soon enough. She had a wardrobe of bed stuff but she slept naked. In the closet were sweet pink bed jackets, long, pink slips with a touch of lace at bottom and around the armholes, fancy stuff with ostrich feathers as kind of a joke. She slept naked, was herself pink, except where fatigue took color from her.

MOM STUFFS TOT IN DRYER

Oriella Sanchez, 28, native of the Dominican Republic, common-law wife of Jorge Santiella, of mixed Hispanic and Italian descent, despondent over gestures made by Mr. Santiella to another woman, locked the door against him. He attempted to force the door down, did force the door down, the door being old, strong where there were locks, but weak otherwise. Police were called. Miss Quality read it on a sheet: the time of the call, who responded. Police took Mr. Santiella from the scene. Miss Sanchez, according to what she told police later, refused to press charges out of fear. Also out of fear (she said), she barricaded herself and her young son in a basement laundry room. Police were called, time of response also on sheet. It was at this point (upon the arrival of the police for the second time) that the headline took place. MOM stuffed TOT (Roberto, 6) in clothes dryer *to hide him*, as she said later to police, all reported on sheet.

Miss Quality sighed.

She turned in bed. Her face was toward the ceiling now. She was roundish and healthy, with big breasts and sweet black curly hair. She passed her hand over her forehead, getting the curly hair back — futile gesture, like asking for patience when your life depends on quickness, or asking for containment when (as with other, blonder women) all the glory of life depends on the movement across your face of long, straight hair that must move with every breeze. Miss Quality brushed aside her curls, knowing they would be back to comfort her.

Miss Quality sighed. *Miss Quality won't be disturbed,* she thought. She was a person from an older time.

RIO

She remembered South America before it got spoiled.

HEIRESS
She knew South American men. Pepito, Juanito, and Baby.

HEIRESS
She knew Miss Henry. Ah, Miss Henry.

She knew Detective Jerry Umder. He was the small, intense kind of cop, eager to be known in restaurants. He followed sports, made bets, bought clothes. Miss Quality placed items sent her way by Detective Umder near to sports-related items, or fashion items. From time to time she mentioned his name: TOP DETECTIVE JERRY UMDER. Every so often, as a treat, she took him to La Primavera, the fashionable restaurant. She had no trouble from Detective Umder.

Detective Umder was a funnel (there were several others) through which certain criminals came into Miss Quality's sphere. Detective Umder had introduced her to Oscar Telemon (DAD DYES DAUGHTER PINK), Celestina Murgen (SEX CHANGE NURSE PULLS THE PLUG), and a series of remarkable children, among them young Jorge Ferlino (PSYCHIC TOT LIVES IN TOXIC WASTE), who had established a community of young people in an abandoned chemical dump. This latter story had won for Miss Quality's newspaper a Crusading Journalism Award.

She turned in bed. *Miss Quality can't be disturbed,* she thought. *Miss Quality is through with rip-off productions that refuse to encourage growth.* She lay on her back. She put a moist hand on her brow. This was quite deliberate. Then, as though all energy had left her, she collapsed out of movement and allowed her hand to fall as a dead weight. Her hand took a route away from her, to the right. It hit a piece of hardwood, lightly sculpted, the seat of a chair. A phrase began out loud and continued in quiet. "Damn," she said out loud, feeling her hand hurt. *Esther*, she said to herself. She turned over, putting her back to the chair.

Time passed. Light came through the curtain. Light changed. It began in white and turned to yellow. It walked along the floor.

The sun advanced on women who were up. It advanced on Esther, who was not up. The room was bright where Esther lay asleep. Its decorative scheme was within view. It was done in an old style — full of curves and blond wood and frosted glass and small cutout motifs: dolphin, wave, palm tree. It was like a child's room. Esther, in bed, was like a child in bed: sweet, round, a little wet. She tumbled about in a child's reluctance.

Then, the last part of reluctance gone, she got up. Naked, she went to the door. She opened the door. *I'm a full-figured gal*, she thought as she bent down. *Full-figured then; full-figured now.* She sighed.

She picked up a newspaper, stood up, moved back inside, and closed the door. She stood still, holding the newspaper. She held it as if it were a wounded cat.

She put the newspaper down on a table and walked, plump and naked, to the bathroom. She washed. She used a washcloth just dampened with water. She didn't like water. She dressed.

At last, she put on a black wool worsted riding jacket. She went to a small jewelry case and took out a small diamond pin. She carefully pinned it to the lapel of the riding jacket. Miss Quality, as her readers knew, believed in classics.

She was dressed, but she was not happy. *The lady; the legend; the truth*, she thought. Then she thought: maybe not the truth. She should call her mother. That was the truth. She was an ungrateful child, that was the truth. She had two friends in the world: a real friend called Galen and an imaginary friend called Miss Henry. What was a thirty-year-old woman doing with an imaginary friend? She sighed. *Nighttime in Rio*, she thought.

She was a victim of phrases. *Nighttime in Rio; The only toothbrush your family will ever need; More than a mint — a miracle.* She remembered them all. She was quick to pick things up.

She looked at herself in the mirror. She did this only once a day. She was dressed, but she was not happy. *Nighttime in Rio*, she thought.

This time with Alice Morgan as the dizzy deb. She does the rumba like a sulky child playing "Nola" on the piano: she speeds it up hoping to get it over with fast. It *is* fast; giddy; but no fun. We end up dizzy but curiously detached. It's a vicarious roller-coaster ride; we infer the movement because we see how motion sick *she* is.

She moved back from the mirror. Sometimes she wanted to look at her legs. Sometimes not.

Randy Turpin as the hotel manager —

She bent over to remove a thread from her skirt.

— the part he played also five years before when the title was *Nevada Decree*.

She moved into the bathroom to deposit the string daintily in the commode. The bathroom, she noted again, needed a good cleaning.

The *first* film version was the Gilda Renn silent *Bombay*. Remade again in 1956 as *Desert Story*.

86

So many times, she thought, sitting down at the table. She sighed, remembering that there was a film by that name too.

When she got up, she had read the morning tabloid, paying especial attention to the "Nina Knows" column.

She left the paper on the table and went out. The hallway was wide. There were no sounds.

She walked down Broadway. She looked at signs. All posters had an interest for her.

Tradewinds
Happy Hour Four to Seven

At the subway kiosk, she bought the early edition of her own newspaper. She waited in line to buy a token. She stood behind a tired-looking black woman who had, also, a copy of her newspaper, which was the *New York Poll.* She followed the black woman through the stile, into the station, and down the narrow stairs to the platform.

She looked at words.

A Kalin-Harven Production
of
A Stanley Aspirf Film

GREY FERMAN

LARRY TRAFFER

SALLY BORNE

in

HARDBALL

A Luricosta Release

87

She shrugged. Larry's the *screwball*, throwing Grey a *curve*, she thought. She moved on. The black woman was now close on her left, the *Poll* in her hand. Aries Richard call John, she thought, remembering something she had seen written on a poster. *Spitball*.

The train came. Esther knew, now, to call the subway the *train*. She used it in her column. Black idiom. She was toying with other instances: *baffroom*, for example, instead of the more conventional "bathroom"; *birffday* for "birthday"; both of these might be effective. *Bowff?* It was hard to decide how far to go.

In the train, she took a seat opposite the black woman. She waited for the black woman to read the *Poll*, or not. The black woman looked straight ahead. Time went by. The woman opened the paper. Miss Quality, nonchalant, opened her paper, too. KILLER SCREAMS FOR MERCY was the big headline on page three, story from page one.

The black woman glanced at the page and moved on. Miss Quality turned the page in her paper. Miss Quality looked to the left-hand page, page four. She began to be fidgety. Calm down, she said to herself. She looked at page four. *So dull*, she thought. Page four was the page for foreign and domestic news. SUPER PREZ RIPS REDS. "Around the World and Nation," as reported by our wire services. Will she read this? She did not look up to see. Bad luck, Miss Quality thought, to look too soon.

The train came into a station. The train stopped. *When it stops, look up*, Miss Quality told herself. The train stopped. Two men and an old woman got on. *Mother*, Miss Quality thought, with anger.

The black woman was reading the Miss Quality column. Esther sat still in her seat. If she reads the first paragraph,

I'll read the first paragraph too, Esther thought. The woman read on and on. Miss Quality felt herself a little moist. She turned her eyes to her own work:

MISS QUALITY

She paused. Still reading? Wonder if *shiv* will stop her? She turned back to the paper.

The hot muggers are the SWEET BOYS, led by Ramon Menendez, 12, a real Quality Act. Ramon, tasting blood on his lip from a rabbit punch thrown by Roberto Venezeluano, reacted with typical SWEET BOY panache, took his small shiv from inside the rabbit's foot he carries at his waist and plunged it into Roberto's eye. Too BAD, but Miss Q loves the *rabbit touch*.

Miss Quality sat silent, hardly breathing. The black woman continued to read. Her hands were a little grey, a little ashy. Miss Quality knew the condition. Her eyes were tired. *Two jobs*, Miss Quality thought. *Anyone in trouble?* The black woman read on, unblinking. Her hand reached up and turned the collar on her coat. The coat was dark in a bad plaid; big weave. *Couldn't be warm*, Miss Quality thought. Why not a better coat? Miss Quality was angry, suddenly, at the coats worn by poverty. The black woman turned the page, leaving Miss Quality behind. The woman began to snooze. Her body rocked hard back and forth. Esther put her paper away. Two stops later she picked it up and read some of the items in the "Around the World and Nation" section; then she took a nap herself. Her own body rocked back and forth with the motion of the train.

Her mouth hung open. A jolt awakened her and she saw that the black woman had gone.

She arrived at the offices of the *Poll*, and took an elevator that was like a freight elevator. It was run by a small bald man with a cigar. It's a *test*, Esther thought. It was her opinion that most things at the *Poll* were *tests*. She passed.

In the city room, Harold Curll, not her friend, had the *Poll* in front of him, pages spread full, each half resting on an open palm, like a Bible would, or a dictionary.

"*But Miss Q loves the rabbit touch*," Harold Curll said solemnly. "For autumn, winter, into spring, let no fur touch your body, but pale, street-killed rabbit — *sorry*," he said, spotting Esther. "My interpolation. But 'street-killed' has a nice ring, don't you think? Useful to you?"

Esther walked past him. Her eyes looked out the windows. Big, dirty windows. They let in grey light. The city room was threaded with different lighting arrangements: early iron fixtures hung from the ceiling, wire encased in metal rods, incandescent bulbs set deep into metal funnels, painted white underneath, now turned grey; newer fixtures, *fluorescent*, were suspended in similar manner, but lacked good iron, were made, instead, of thin steel and plastic, were not funnel-shaped, but like trays for ice. There were lamps as well, set around the groups of wooden desks pushed together, but none of these overcame the diffusion of grey light coming in through the windows.

Curll continued to talk, but Miss Quality put him out of her mind. A leftover, a drunk. What he had left was *speed* and a way with words. His point of view was dated, however, and were it allowed to influence the paper, the paper would fail, Miss Quality thought.

At times, however, Curll would not be denied. He

would go on and on until he succeeded in getting her attention. It could be inconvenient. She looked up. He bloomed. He blew up. His speech, enriched by her looking at him, grew more florid.

"As I say," he said, as though starting again over a noisy but impressionable audience, "the history of the culture, or rather, the trick by which a person may enter the history of the culture, is: steal from niggers." He smiled; he paused. His lower lip, which was, strangely, much larger than the upper, fell away from his teeth, which were stained. This was his smile: he allowed his big lower lip to fall away to reveal his teeth. He smiled, thus, and waited to see: *what effect*. A Negro associate kept on at his typewriter, hearing nothing. Miss Quality looked at Curll steadily. *Drinking problem*, she thought. Curll, gathering second wind, hoisted up his lip, reached around him, uncovered a pack of mentholated cigarettes from under four books of copy on a policeman's funeral, took a cigarette indifferently, as though it had been pressed on him (who took it not wishing to offend). He lit the cigarette. He looked up, addressed the ceiling. "To steal from niggers, of whatever persuasion, what they have that they do not sufficiently value." He paused; puffed on the cigarette with seeming contentment. "We have their music, but frankly, we have grown a little bored with it. What do they have left that we might have the use of — apart from poverty itself, which, thank you very much, they are welcome to?" He paused, waiting for an answer from a dull class. Slowly, he put the index finger of his right hand to the digits of his left, in turn, as though counting something with difficulty. The finger moved from finger to finger, and then he contrived a big, bright look up. "Ah!" he said; the sum revealed. "They have the integrity of their *criminality*, the last strong place wherein they may guard their pride, their secret language."

"Why don't you go and have a *drink*," Miss Quality said.

Starret laughed. Starret was a remarkable figure. He was no more than five foot two. He always wore shiny clothes. He was unable to write or to remember facts. He was kept on, perhaps, because of the way he looked and the unease he created, or because he was regarded as *very American* by the Canadian proprietor of the paper. Esther felt his presence. She looked down at her desk. Her head came close to the desk. There was reason for this in a slight myopia of hers, but also in her fear of Starret. Starret, since he did not write, could not be bought off with words or intimidated by forceful words or innuendo. His ignorance was his weapon. He did not know, for instance, that there was any difference between what she did and what any other columnist did. He told her long stories about the betting habits of columnists he had known (he took them to the track), and he rolled off the names of old floozies they used to take on their arm, as though these people must be known to all columnists. "You know who I saw," he'd say, looking at her with his expression of no under-standing, "*Sally Grey.*"

At last, Esther looked up at him. He was wearing a thin, greasy tie. Esther had recently come down hard on these ties. He winked. He stood perfectly still, as though he were going to stare at her forever, unwelcome guardian. Then he said: "Got a visitor." Esther looked quickly around the room and could see no visitor. She went back to looking at her desk. Time passed. Starret left, but then came back. He stood behind her. She turned around.

"So what do you want me to do with your visitor?" he asked. "Throw her out or what?"

Curll was in earshot. He held up his hand; silence to the room. *All this starting again?* Esther thought. She got up, pushed her chair back hard, almost hitting Starret, this her intention. "Sorry," she said. Brush-back pitch. "I'll see her outside." She followed Starret down the room, out into the hall. *Bad. Bad,* she thought. At times, all her work deserted her. *It goes so slowly,* she thought, thinking of putting one piece of work (her good wool worsted jacket) on top of another. Suddenly she thought of sickrooms. *Your mother's hair has fallen out. Will you see her now?* She came out into the hall and felt cold. Heat came from a gas blower close to the ceiling. It wasn't on. Across the hall was the men's room. Starret came to rest just at the door of it. His standing was stupid and sure. It's the men's room; I have every right to be here, his stance said. All day if I want.

Esther turned her head. She was at the peak of a triangle. Starret was down a line to her right. Down a short, strong line, leading from herself, in a good wool worsted jacket (little diamond pin), was a thin girl, shaved head, sitting on a wooden bench. Like the chair in Esther's room, the bench was solid hardwood, sculpted to receive an ample human body. The girl sat in it like a small package, bony edges biting into the curved wood. Esther moved quickly toward her, blocking Starret's view. "Oh, hello," she said with force, as though it were an appointment properly made they were in, momentarily forgotten by herself. "Why don't we talk in *here*."

Esther led the girl into the women's room, horrible place. There was a big window, two big panes, one on top of the other, metal sash, coated with grime; on the outside of the window an arrangement of strong wire was visible: wire crossing wire into diamond shapes. Strong grey light came in. It was light strong enough to read the smallest print by, but it was grey. Esther and the girl stood still. Conspirators. Would they smoke a cigarette? The girl withdrew from the conspiracy. Applicant. Hostile applicant, Esther thought. The new invitations, Miss Quality thought: come if you dare. The new application: give it here.

The girl said: "We started with the rabbits."

Miss Quality looked. The girl was dressed in kind of a smock, something with a surgical feel, all cotton, maybe, but ordinary cotton, to which various bits of fur had been pinned. The girl said:

I'll tell you how it was. Sweet Boys full of shit. Sweet Boys don't know shit. They just jive, tryin to make a name. Franzy cool, Joey cool, Biggy cool. All down at Elderad, number two, and Freezy's. Freezy said: Jump up at Elder's So Bobby say: Cool first, then jump up. So we cooled. Then little Ab and Jerome get heavy. Jerome say Ab fussin wid him. Jerome say: Cut your ear off stuff it where you hurt. Ab say: Make me hurt; so Jerome make him hurt. Jerome with me after that. So, Jerome and me go jump up. Jerome buy me thing. Everybody know I with Jerome. We go sleep at where his mother's at. She don't know. We *slip in*. So, I and Jerome, real close. I and Jerome move close. I look out back, got this little bitty *cage*. His mother don't fuss with it. Little bitty cage. Jerome show me: Silky, Smoothy, Whitey, Room, little baby bunnies. Jerome, he take out shib, cut Silky. Now you with *me*, Jerome say. I just look. Jerome show me dead Silky. Give it here, I say. That way I get her name.

94

Miss Quality took the girl into the city room. Starret wasn't in the hall, nor was he in the city room. Curll, smoking, his small back curved over his typewriter, looked subdued. Miss Quality thought: she said *shib*; I wonder should I spell it that way? She took the girl with her to her desk. She stood the girl up just where Starret had stood. No one looked. Curll was hunched over. *Afraid*, Miss Quality thought. Funny how they know. Then, hands poised over the typewriter, she thought: No. Correction. Not come if you dare. Come if you think we really want you.

⁓❦ 6 ❧⁓

The Last Mrs. Aspair

"Oh, my little sweetie pie! How you do do a thing — the way you do — that *hair!*" The last Mrs. Aspair stroked Victoria Feldman's hair, which (thick and tangled) had been pulled over from one side of her head (and the back of her head) to the other side, and a comb stuck in it. It was not hard to do if you did it just right. Victoria, loving her hair, had done it right. Her own hand went up so as to see: *Still all right?* To tell the truth, the stroke given by Mrs. Aspair, although it had lasted a very short time, had not been welcomed by Victoria, as she didn't like people fussing with her hair once it had been arranged, and she was afraid that she may have shied away a bit during the moment Mrs. Aspair was touching her, and *this* (the thought that she had, perhaps, failed to be charming) would have caused her to fret (over the question: *Did she notice?*) except that by the time she had the beginning of the thought, Mrs. Aspair had moved on to another guest.

Victoria followed the progress of her hostess around the

room. Mrs. Aspair took, at every opportunity, an unexpected turn. It was her special way. In talking, she jumped over words to a word much ahead of the one she might have been expected to utter, then headed off from *that* one in a direction a person would not have thought to predict (unless that person knew her well, that is — which is to say, met her more than once, in which case he did predict it); in walking, she almost *limped*. These small awkwardnesses implied *impatience*, evidence of an active will betrayed by the frailties of age (this is what she said it was) or by the inability of mere movement or mere language to encompass the ferocious energy of her intent (this is what she meant her friends to think). She was apt to bring the subject up. "Oh, they ought to shoot me! They ought to do me — I shouldn't mind it — like a horse!" was something she had said more than once. And (more than once) she had said gravely: "Do you know, I am a very stupid old woman. I still *run ahead*, you see. I've done it all my life. Dear Sixte used to say, 'Sophie has more energy than she can consume locally,' which was wicked of Sixte, but true — and now you see what my legs are and my poor mind." Saying this (and she had said it more than once, just this way), she would hang her head a little to one side and keep it there, out of tiredness, perhaps, or to show sincerity. The hang of the head seemed to say: see, it's not all fun with me. It brought a person closer. Perhaps a person moved closer. A person noticed that when Sophie's head was hung to one side, she did not stumble or jump in talking or abbreviate her sentences. Room was left, as it is in ordinary discourse, for response. Her friends knew what to say.

My dear, your mind — I wish *I* had your mind

was one response appropriate to be made to Sophie's hanging head. A better one, made by those who knew better how to affect simplicity, was: *quiet*, first. (Beat, beat, beat.) Then:

No one knows what you do, Sophie.

These were special, private moments. They ended in quiet. And then Sophie Aspair would bring her head up, and then she was almost certain to say as she *gathered* something in her hands — something, anything, perhaps a handbag, perhaps a report given to her by a man in government or at her foundation (for Sophie was very active and did not believe it was modern to sponsor a gathering at which no real business was done) — she was almost certain to say, just at the moment before her composure had been utterly restored: "And of course I miss Sixte dreadfully."

Victoria smiled. Mrs. Aspair faded across the room. Victoria again touched her hand to her hair. *I could live here*, she thought. *I could spend my life standing here.* Her thought was, perhaps, the remnant of prudence. She was descended from prudence. Of her ancestor Samuel Smuyt (New Englander come to New York) it was said that "he did not commit the impropriety of paying large wages"; and Gerrit Anthor, compiler of *The Rich Men of New-York*, was not surprised to find "the richest man in America" — her ancestor, the first Johannes Aspair — "looking over a ledger-book in an office in Prince Street." Prudence descended and was shaped by events. Victoria Feldman kept watch over her last asset: her friendship with Sophie Aspair.

The rooms were almost crowded. They were filling up,

and as they filled, Sophie became more and more agitated. She ran to the small room where men and women entered. She ran back to the drawing room, where men and women came to rest. Above the rising energy of her party, she rose higher still. Certain established men and women, coming into the drawing room, moved slowly, sought a favorite corner in which to stand (for very few people were so secure in their position at Sophie's that they actually would *sit*, so early in the evening), and, all in all, seemed to say, to anyone who took the trouble to look, *we know this house very well*. Sophie, on the other hand, seemed to be discovering it for the first time. Had she just moved in, she could not have been so vague about where things properly were to be. She did not seem to know where she should be *herself*, so at times it seemed that the party must be breaking up, not forming, and under the burden of some emergency.

It was, in fact, a whim of Sophie's that her dinners should have about them the energy of *the crisis*, and to this end she applied to each event within her evening (and then, again, over these events, to the evening as a whole) a rhythm of: problem, problem, *solution* — so that even so simple a matter as the greeting of guests was inserted into a scheme of *crisis management* (a phrase she knew from men in government) in which the spotting of the guest (*once, twice*) was made into the problem and some physical gesture of greeting (kiss, pat, mock-blow) into the solution; and this was in harmony with the long rhythm of the evening, in which the frenzy of the greeting period rose to a climax over a dinner so loud with discussion that it began to seem like a panic, until, at last, *solution* was reached in *quiet*, a *hush* that descended (final results announced) as the company abandoned dinner for the drawing room, where *space* and *quiet* were set out and in which an important man found an opportunity to discuss a *real* crisis — for just as other women bearing the name *Mrs. Aspair* had given dances or had musicians in, Sophie, the last to have the name, invited in men who were not afraid of emergencies.

Sophie was called the last Mrs. Aspair, but of course there were others. It was a large family. There were many Aspairs, some bearing the old names: Johannes, James-James, Petrus, Corneil, but the family had lost its sense of proportion. Some branches had bloomed with children and grown poor; others had stayed rich, grown richer, but *narrowed* until, as in the example of Sophie's dead husband Sixte, they came to an end in a man who declined to have children at all. "I've had *wives*," Sixte Aspair said, putting the issue to a stop.

So he did have. He had three before Sophie: two sisters and Lila Codman in the middle. Lila Codman had put the experience away, but the two sisters, living still, amused themselves, if that was what it was, by using their names, married and maiden, in a kind of rotation, the pattern of which was theirs alone to know, so that one or the other would turn up, from time to time, as "Mrs. Sixte Aspair," on the list of a charity bazaar or something worse, which was the next thing to fraud, as Sophie thought. But this was nothing next to the inflation of the name caused by Sixte's cousin Jim-Jim, who married and married again, until, Sophie said, she stopped counting. Shopkeepers had learned not to give credit to the name and it had been many years since Sophie had been polite to any woman presenting herself as "your cousin Mrs. James-James Aspair." Jim-Jim had had just one respectable wife, the first, his cousin Beata Aspair; and this woman — Mrs.

Aspair-Feldman-Belsorsky-Post (Beata Aspair), as she was in the Social Register — lived under Sophie's domination. No one laughed more than this faded woman did when Sophie told a story at the expense of the Mrs. Jim-Jims and the ex–Mrs. Sixtes; no one was more insistent that Sophie was the last Mrs. Aspair worthy of the name.

Mrs. Aspair-Feldman-Belsorsky-Post was in the room. Victoria Feldman, her daughter, saw her and avoided her.

Besides her mother and Sophie, there were other relatives and connections in the room. Some of them were not attractive. Victoria, looking around, saw a few that were, in a way, repulsive. But Sophie Aspair did not seem to mind and she had a special way, and perhaps a use, too, for each one. Now, for instance, she came past obese, slack-jawed Van Horne Aspair and *winked.* She winked and then hit him a little blow on the back. Van Aspair grinned, and for a moment you could see into his mouth. Then he said: "Damn you, Sophie, why can't a fellow get a good drink in this house?" and he made a grimace, a kind of pout. His eyebrows came together, his cheeks bulged out, and his mouth, his vast mouth, stretched almost from ear to ear. It was an unusual expression, almost an *accomplishment,* and the spirit in which it was offered was unusual as well. He offered the pout as something to please a crowd (as perhaps it had, once, in the nursery) and as something to enforce caste. Perhaps Sophie accepted it in this spirit; certainly she took his rude gesture in stride, saying merely: "No, you can't be, not tonight — horrible!"

Victoria might have continued to follow Sophie's progress except that a young man almost bumped into her. She did not see him coming. She had the impression of a nearly missed connection: . . . *but for that I would have been crushed. The plane had just taken off — imagine: that was the one that crashed.* The moment was within the spirit of the accidental. He was acting within an impersonal rhythm of movement. Rather like me on the street, Victoria thought.

She watched him. He was dressed in the style of a young man in business: his suit was of the glenurquhart plaid that young men in business sometimes wear; he was sandy-haired; he wore eyeglasses with a clear plastic frame. He was unremarkable in every way. A stranger in Sophie's rooms would have seen him and thought: good family, yes; good schools, yes; just the sort of man who would be here, *certainly.* Victoria, who knew these rooms very well, knew at once that he had come without an invitation.

He was the sort of person Sophie never did ask. Sophie was like the head of an Islamic sect living in Paris: she accepted the tribute of the Traditional People who had set her up in business, but she declined to know them socially. There were two reasons for this, opposite and balanced.

First of all, she liked to *work at* being Mrs. Aspair and found herself ill at ease among people who gave her their allegiance out of respect for her merely existing; second, she did not know the ramifications of the group as well as the head of the group should know them (she having entered into it rather late), and she did not like the idea that there should be in her rooms people who knew more than she did about what she was supposed to represent.

So, she was quite careful about which of her clan she asked, more careful than anyone suspected, except Victoria, who had come to understand that the welcome held out to her (and to her mother, for instance, and Van Aspair) was extended so that she and certain other unthreatening members of the Family might represent all the Traditional People who were absent.

So, the young man had not been invited. He might have come with someone who had been invited, except that Sophie did not encourage this, and, in any case, he seemed to be quite alone.

Victoria smiled her best smile. It created distance if distance was needed, or intimacy if distance needed to be bridged. It brought energy to her skin and a force of radiance to the place where she was standing. It had been with her always, this smile. When she was a child it had been the smile of a beautiful child; when a girl coming of age, it had been the smile of a charming young girl; now it was beautiful and womanly. It had been with her always, and at all ages it had been a protection — protection for her, a gift for other persons, best protection when it was offered with best feeling, as now. *For you?* she wondered.

From across the room the young man confused her smile with a conventional smile. But he did think: what a pretty girl.

She continued to watch him. He *touched* things. He picked things up and put them down again, moving, moving. *They will think he is stealing,* Victoria thought. But no one noticed him, because a change had come over the room. It had *parted.* A man entered who represented *the work of the moment.* The work of the moment flowed through him. The work of the moment was going on somewhere else (in an office, somewhere underground, on an airplane in midflight) and yet this man, its representative, was *here.* Sophie saw him. She loved work. She was honest about it. She was honest in general. She was honest about her *love of work* and her *love of family* and her *open mind.* At her parties, representatives of these three estates met as in a parliament, and the opportunities for give-and-take implicit in the situation were carefully cultivated, which was healthy and democratic; and yet: each guest left in the estate he came in.

The estate of work was in ascendance now. The men who had the power to part the room now were new men who had the knack of seeming old. They came, a little harried, straight from their offices — which were special offices, often, set up to rectify the mistakes made by others. The men who occupied the foreground at Mrs. Aspair's, now, rarely held *elective* office, as they were too good ever to be elected. The space given over to these men encroached on the space that had been (at one time) reserved for men of *open mind* and for those whose presence suggested openness of mind in others, but this was a natural result of the unfolding of events, and Mrs. Aspair, however stern she was in some ways, did not oppose the unfolding of events.

The man who had parted the room was small and thin and dark, and it was obvious that he had not had time to change clothes or shave or prepare in any other way for his evening engagement. This he seemed to bear rather as a badge of honor than an embarrassment, for when Mrs. Aspair came up to him in welcome, he was not diffident at all, but pressed his unshaven cheek to her cheek. He was seen to whisper something in her ear. Immediately as this was done she jumped back and exclaimed, "Max, you're wicked! Wicked!" She did not say this in a coquettish voice at all but rather in a tone that implied that *she* would be a friend whatever foolish people thought. Keeping this tone, and repeating the word *wicked* from moment to moment, sometimes using a shake of the head, she guided the small, dark man through the crowd without taking the slightest notice of anyone, and took him out of the room through a small door, defying anyone not to see how quickly she might, in the proper circumstances, discard all ceremony. In a minute she came out again, shaking her head still, still uttering a weak *wicked* at intervals. She went back across the room again, head down. Head down, she took a glass from a tray of glasses. Head down, she went to a carved standing chest. Ignoring and circumventing the attractive young men she had hired to circulate through the drawing room taking orders for drinks, she opened the chest and took out a bottle of whiskey. She poured a large amount into the glass. She looked up and addressed everyone and no one. "You see how he looks," she said without her friendly stutter. "He really shouldn't have come at all."

Victoria was suddenly less at ease. The entrance of the small, dark man had been very abrupt. It had halted certain slow developments. She stood perfectly still. She did not smile, because she honored her smile and wished to preserve its power. A smile without any motive behind it but the counteracting of fear was a violation, she felt, with a price to be paid later. The thing to do with fear was to wait it out quietly. The *overt* fathered fear in Victoria. She did not like it when the decks were cleared. She did not like the phrase "That's all very well," for instance. When people said, "That's all very well, but we must be more realistic now" (and her cousin and benefactress Mrs. Aspair *had* said this), she felt that she had been wrapped up in the "all very well," and killed off. When an overt action suddenly overpowered the small, comfortable movements she had begun to establish, she said to herself, always: *What will they do to me?* She thought that now; she stopped and stayed perfectly still; she forgot the young man altogether.

She did not think about him at dinner. The din was fearsome. She wanted to cover her ears. Sophie's guests, knowing what was expected, vied with one another: louder and louder. Opinions were expressed. Opinions were shouted.

"No, you can't — impossible!" Sophie shouted over the racket, raising the tempo. What was said? It was hard to remember. Each guest spoke from his own past. He reached back to the last opinion he had held successfully and shouted that. Each one thought: When was I not embarrassed? Some people had to go back quite far. Van Aspair took himself back to the high-ceilinged nursery of his parents' house in Brookline. He threw his face up into a pout. He threw his fists down on the table. He sought to terrorize the maids.

The food was not quickly renewed. Plates, empty of nourishment, were not replaced. On plates where food had been, small juices congealed: echo of rack of lamb; liquor of peas and asparagus, remnant of butter, and ichor of fish. Bread remained. Did any guest, in the heat of *good talk*, so forget himself that his hand found good stuff in: melted butter, blood, essence of fish, all mopped up by bread? Possibly, but only because the talk was so good, the atmosphere so heady with ideas and so intersected with shouts and screeches of conviction that it was hard to remember that one was not at home.

The Governor of the state, annoyed that the room no longer parted for him, predicted economic collapse. His wife, on the other hand, looked forward to increased

THE LAST MRS. ASPAIR

profitability. Thinking of tenements, she said: "The numbers are great. All you've got to worry about is *evictions*. Somehow you have to get those oldsters out."

"Creative renovation is the key," her dinner partner said.

"If you can get the dead weight out," the Governor's wife said, looking wistfully at a serving dish that held just one pea coated in a delicate glaze of remnant of butter. "And I mean *if*."

Victoria's mother, Mrs. Aspair-Feldman-Bolsorsky-Post, was a little drunk. As always, when she was drunk, she talked about herself. "I was married to two of the richest men in America," she said, looking her dinner partner straight in the eye (but not seeing him). She began at the beginning. "I was born Aspair, and I married Aspair," she said significantly. "Like the Double Duchess."

Her partner made no response.

"The Double Duchess. Didn't you ever hear of the Double Duchess?" She was belligerent, then, suddenly, she was almost studious. She put the index finger of her right hand to the index finger of her left hand, as though doing a sum. "First she was Sutherland . . ."

"No, Manchester," a woman said from two places away.

"That's right, *Manchester*," Mrs. Post said, relieved to have the right name, but annoyed too. She looked at her plate. It was full. She didn't eat when she drank. She didn't believe in it. "Anyway, *she's* not the point," Mrs. Post said, a little sad, "*I'm* the point. I was born Aspair. And I married Aspair."

"It's true," the woman two places away said gently. "Mrs. Post has been married to a number of prominent men."

Mrs. Post looked up. "That's right," she said. Then

she looked at the woman. Mrs. Post was myopic. She did not wear glasses. She squinted. "Why, it's Nina," she said, almost sweetly.

Nina, who wrote the syndicated gossip column "Nina Knows," adopted the soothing tone of a nurse. She said, "Yes, dear, it's Nina." Mrs. Post calmed down. Nina entered the conversation. She explained Mrs. Post to the young man who was Mrs. Post's dinner partner, and she explained Mrs. Post to herself. It was medicine. They took it and calmed right down.

"Mrs. Post was a glamour debutante," Nina said. "She did endorsements for Jural cigarettes and Horvey's face cream, just like movie stars did. She was married to James-James Aspair in the wedding of the year in 1936. She had a heartbreaking divorce, which was all over the front pages when she accused Jim-Jim of having intimate relations with Franny de la Perealt on the Twentieth Century Limited."

"That tramp," Mrs. Post said with feeling. She began to pick at her food.

"She won a Nevada decree and married on the rebound."

"Feldman was my fling," Mrs. Post said, looking with interest at a piece of lamb.

"It didn't work out, of course, and two years later Mrs. Post sought a separation, and then a divorce, charging mental cruelty."

"He wasn't cruel, actually," Mrs. Post said. "Just crazy."

Nina, who knew it was important to move with the times, cut the story short. "Later, Mrs. Post married a Russian prince and after that a sportsman."

"*That* pig," Mrs. Post said. "I want you to print something about him."

Nina said of course she would. The young man, who

had listened patiently, now was a little alarmed to see that Mrs. Post, showing a renewed interest in life, was beginning to address herself to her meal, some of which he had hoped to get for himself. Seeing his chance, he asked: "I wonder if I could have one of your potatoes?"

Dinner dispersed. Women reached for their little bags. Had hair held up? Had violent talk dispersed the color on lips and cheeks? Women stole a glance: reflection? Mirror? Women moved toward mirrors. Around a small room where many mirrors were spread out — where mirror unfolded on mirror; where every aspect could be seen; where opportunities were fresh, and examination promised improvement — around this small room, guarded by a small French-seeming chair, there formed — a line. Seeing it — the line — Victoria thought *no no*, and then: *must have a little hit*, meaning cocaine.

She looked about her. Men and women had moved into the drawing room. Everyone? Two men lingered at a table, their talk too good to admit of interruption. Victoria lingered with them, standing. If the room were to empty, even for a moment, well, her movements could be very quick. The room did not empty. Talk continued.

"He offended the wrong lady."

". . . where the bodies are buried."

"Media pressure."

Victoria lingered. *Must have a little hit*, she thought. The talkers did not leave. Maids entered. With grim efficiency they took away dishes, silverware, linen, revealing naked tables. These (except for the one at which the talkers were seated) they folded up. Caterer's stuff. They took the chairs and stacked them. *Stacked them?* Yes. *What were these chairs like?* They were small, collapsible, with little, red, velvetlike bottoms. *Had they been rented?* No. Sophie, remembering advice from a more simple time in her life, thought: Why rent when you can buy? Locating a caterer's supply establishment, she bought them. *Were there no good chairs passing down from generation to generation within the Aspair family?* Not in this branch. Sixte Aspair once had a set of "modern" chairs at his house in New York, but Sophie didn't like them and they were discarded. He had, also, an enormous set of rather ugly French-seeming chairs, come to him from his mother, which he kept at his house in Rhode Island. One of these had been retained by Sophie and was sitting now nearby the waiting women. The others (together with the rest of the contents of the Rhode Island house) had been sold at auction, where they fetched a very low price. *Did Mrs. Aspair not know a good chair from a bad chair?* She did know. Good chairs were pointed out to her — and she bought them. They passed directly from the seller to a museum, however, without stopping at her house.

Victoria thought: Will they notice? The two men were deep in discussion. They had not looked her way. Her movements could be very quick. Still, she thought, *better not.* She moved. Her long legs took her through the room, past the men in discussion. Through a door, she found herself in a hallway. Here? Better not, she thought. She went to the left. Here was another door. Passing through it, she came to a small room adjacent to the drawing room — the library. To the left was the drawing room, where men and women grew quiet now. To the right — a door to Sophie's bedroom. Quickly, Victoria entered here and found: Sophie, shoe off, leg tucked under her, sitting on small love seat, head over, listening to Max (seated on small footstool, head forward, intent). Victoria did not miss a beat. She said: "Darling, darling, please forgive — there's a ghastly *line* at the one outside and . . ." With the confidence of a sweet child, she rushed to Sophie, gave her a little kiss on the forehead, and went past her to *the little girls' room*, shutting door, reaching bag, taking package, opening, scooping, sniffing. It used to be that I could do that all the time, Victoria thought, thinking of her easy movement, thinking: what a good girl, thinking (stuff all put back in bag), *now I shall be very bright.*

Sophie looked up as Victoria passed through the room again. Victoria did not speak. Victoria, head down, walked straight ahead, as if to say: too polite to interrupt. Sophie thought: didn't take her very long. Then she thought: no more lipstick on her now than when she went in. Thinking this, she lost the thread of what she was hearing.

Max said: "The only solution that makes sense at all is *incapacitation.*"

Sophie lost the thread but heard the word. Her mind sought to spin the thread out of the word ("oh, my mind . . . my poor mind"), but she could not immediately do it. She knew they were talking about Negroes. She had spent much of the last twenty years talking about Negroes. *Incapacitation.* Suddenly she remembered. Words came back to her: *deprived; institutionalized racism; multiservice approach.* She picked up the thread.

"Of course they're incapacitated. Because of institutionalized racism."

Max made no response. Looked. Sophie went on.

"Which is why we must have a multiservice approach."

Max looked. Sophie saw: wrong thread. ("Oh, my poor mind!") Not multiservice approach. Some other approach.

Which approach? She spent a moment in confusion, terrible balance of the moments she spent in the counterfeit of confusion. Retreating, she found: Mrs. Aspair, last voice of New York. "But it's very rude of me to keep you all to myself and now we really must join the others," she said. Passing into the drawing room, she thought: *damn Victoria anyway.*

Entering the drawing room, Victoria, bright, saw the young man. He stood against the wall, facing what must be, inevitably, the seat Max would take. This was a small barrel-backed chair, covered in light blue velvet; it stood by itself away from the wall opposite the young man, angled to face much of the room. The young man looked secure in his position. He looked like a fan does who knows the best cheap seat. *He's been here before,* Victoria thought.

Max came in. He stood by the chair. He seemed to say: we are the last group (no one had left); he seemed to say: we are a very small group (the group was very large); he seemed to say: we know one another well (very few people knew more than a few others well); he seemed to say (and this was the conceit upon which all the others rested): *we are the heirs . . .*

Were they the heirs? Possibly not. But there was an *inheritance*, certainly. The Columbia River, teeming with fish, for one thing. Also: a scheme to water stock. Also *title*, free and clear, to: No. 78 Pearl Street; No. 330 Broadway; the Cozfen Farm (encompassing the land from Sixth Avenue to the river, Fourteenth Street to Thirtieth Street, inclusive, corresponding almost exactly to the area later called the Ninth Ward, with the northern part of the Seventh Ward thrown in); Spuyterkill, a modest house on the Hudson River just above Tarrytown (now supervised by the National Conservators' Council

— open to the public); Land View, a larger place on
Bellevue Avenue, Newport, Rhode Island (now home to
Carmelite Sisters, eager to leave); No. 220 Fifth Avenue
(torn down); No. 880 Fifth Avenue (national headquarters of the National Suicide Prevention Bureau); the
Aspair Court Apartments (U-shaped, entrance for carriages, of Indiana limestone, echo of Italy, built to last,
Lenox Avenue and 120th Street). One might mention
the criminals currently in residence at the Aspair Court
Apartments, and the politicians formerly at home within
the Ninth Ward. Also, well-beloved figures from the
Family: Mrs. James-James II (Ama Stone), who had
ruled in New York and Newport, and young Johannes IV,
dripping in seaweed, who went down on the *Titanic*.
There was an inheritance in the Arts. There was a charming portrait of Mrs. James-James III by Boldini; an appealing family grouping (artist unknown) of Johannes II,
his wife, and children in the old Broadway house (burned
then demolished); a more formal presentation of the
James-James II family in the ballroom of their house at
220 Fifth Avenue (demolished); and a most unusual
primitive (most rare and valuable) of the founder,
Johannes I, with a hookah, chicken, and ducks. As for
Literature, one had a choice of ledgers, mortgage-books,
deeds, covenants, wills, lawsuits, press clippings, marriage
contracts, decrees of divorce, headlines, reports, files, white
papers, blue books, red books, purple books, and fine
morocco bindings. Special note might be made of a complete (and valuable) set of *Secrets of the Courts of
Europe* by M. deVoudin; multiple listings in the Social
Register (Mrs. Aspair-Feldman-Bolsorsky-Post — Beata
Aspair); a volume of verse (*A Passage to Arcady*) by the
ethereal Alice-Marie Aspair; a work of science fiction (un-

published) by Sixte's father, the mechanically minded Johannes III, entitled "A Voyage to Pluto by Rail"; notebooks; examination papers; character sketches; scraps of doggerel; and a listing in *The Rich Men of New-York*, viz:

ASPAIR, JOHANNES

Johannes Aspair is classed by those who know him best as not only the richest, but among the greatest men living in America. It is a *canard* that we must seek today for the spirit of energy which in older days found its characteristic expression in the work of the soldier and the evangelizing missionary, not in the battlefield or the cloister, but in the counting-house, where commercial endeavors unexampled in the history of the world are, at this moment, greeted in our metropolis with a calm acceptance, which is the more remarkable as the endeavors realized are large. This *acceptance* must not be confused with the *languors* or *passivities* encountered among other races; it is, rather, an expression of the *confidence* which has slowly and justly formed over work which seeks to yoke and harness the turbulent confluences of our new continent, and this *confidence* is but the natural result of an *understanding* which has dawned on certain men of our day, of how large the future of the country must be and how overflowing must be the stream of wealth issuing from it. Among these men of *understanding* who have seen and understood the power of the stream and who have, in quiet, made their decision to ride it, and yes, even to master it, Johannes Aspair stands supreme. Born into poverty in his native Scotland, he saw in his youth the constrictions of a life bounded around by material want, and his first ambition, as legend has it, was formed before he could read, and that was: *to be as rich as Squire Ferdon*. The extent today of the fortune of the good family of Ferdon is unknown to us, but we must hazard the guess that Johannes Aspair has made good his boast, for his fortune is estimated to have reached thirty millions of dollars — an incalculable sum, the largest accumulation of wealth on this continent, rivalled in all the world, in all probability, only by the properties held by the Crowned Heads, a few Grandees and Magnates, and by two or three of England's richest Dukes. And consider: these aristocratic fortunes just mentioned, accumulated over a lengthy time — centuries in most examples — represent what? Nothing but the multiplied misery of entire peoples, for they have been put together through coercion, through the subjugation of rural places and the *robbery* of the wealth of the town. And to what end? So that good land may lie unproductive through old-fashioned management (which none may dare change lest *change*, the ancient enemy of privilege, spread through contagion to infect the very structure of privilege itself); so that a *great dead weight* may lie on all the natural faculties of men. How different a picture is presented by Mr. Aspair, working unfettered in a new land. His own manner is simple. His house in Broadway is ample but unpretending. He keeps a carriage, it is true, but for the pleasure and healthful qualities a ride in the open will bring to his wife and sons. He himself prefers to walk, and his small, trim figure is well known to those who frequent the district between his house in Broadway and his office at the corner of Prince and Mercer Streets. Those who know the habits of Dukes and Princes would be surprised, perhaps, to find the richest man in America looking over a ledger-book in an office in Prince Street, but his fellow citizens are not astonished at this sight (which may be seen six days out of seven), and know that far from seeking to impose the *great dead weight* of privilege upon his fellow men, Mr. Aspair has ever sought

115

to *uplift* them, subscribing to many charitable efforts to that end. And in what lies his wealth? Not in castles and tenantries (which, however high a value they may be estimated to have, may have, in fact, no value at all if no *buyer* can be found for them), but in metropolitan real estate, which every day increases in value, and in ready money. . . .

There *were* heirs in the room. They had their thoughts.
Do I have money for a taxi? Victoria Feldman wondered, brightness fading. Fear, then, of looking in her purse.

If Nina prints something in her column maybe Post will hurry up with that check, Mrs. Aspair-Feldman-Bolsorsky-Post thought. *Damn his great pig hide.* She took a cigarette and lit it.

The inheritance was all around: the marriages of Mrs. Post, the great pout of Van Aspair. Nina saw it all. She looked at Mrs. Post, who was lighting a cigarette in her special way. What an awful woman, Nina thought. And yet . . . (she thought of herself, age ten, looking up from a rotogravure: *Aspair-Aspair. Marriage of the year*). Well, Nina thought, *she had a little something.*

Max sat in the chair reserved for him. Sophie sat nearby. He began to talk. He talked about Negroes and crime and something he called "the narrowing of progress." This was a phrase he had invented. He had been pleased, recently, to see it used in one or two serious journals.

For example [*he said*], when the country moved from horses to mechanized transport, it was possible to promise that everyone who had had benefit from a horse would have a *greater benefit* from the specific form of mechanized transport that would be allotted to him — a car or a truck — and an indirect benefit, greater still, from the increase in overall wealth made possible by the switch.

[*Pause*]

For instance, let us take, as a not very typical example, our hostess Sophie.

[*A little amused laughter*]

In the older circumstance I described, I would be able to promise, let us say, that if Mrs. Aspair agreed to give me

[*Violation of personal space: Max touched Sophie's neck*]

that handsome necklace — rubies is it?

[*No answer*]

Let's say rubies — that I would agree to give her back *right here and now* an even better necklace of rubies and diamonds *plus*

[*Holds up finger*]

I would promise to put a sum of money in the bank in her name sufficient to insure the education to her children.

[*Pause*]

This has changed now.

[*Pause*]

What has changed is the *right here and now*. As *progress narrows*, I am still able to promise that if you give up certain things, I will be able to give you back something of greater value — but I don't have any way of making a *direct* exchange. I can guarantee that the *indirect* benefit — the increase in overall wealth — will be sufficient to insure a happy circumstance: i.e., progress; but the direct benefit — i.e., a ruby and diamond necklace for Sophie — has disappeared.

117

[*Giggles*]

But of course, I'm not talking about necklaces. What I'm talking about is employment. Jobs. As *progress narrows* we are going to find ourselves in a position where we are going to have to say: you give me your horse (your job), but you are not going to get a specific allotment of mechanized transportation back. What you are going to get back is a piece of the increased overall wealth made possible by the switch we are making, which is, in this case, to various technological systems that are not labor-intensive.

[*Pause*]

This is what I have been discussing with that genial man, the President of the United States.

[*Smiles*]

Max paused. He shifted his feet. Other people released themselves from the positions they were in. Sophie sighed. This had gone on for longer than was really comfortable. Where were the Negroes in this? She felt, what she rarely felt, an ebbing of *verve*. She moved in her chair. Max went on. She did not concentrate. *I liked the multiservice approach*, she thought dreamily. What was wrong with it? Her mind wandered to afternoons spent in Harlem, opening cafeterias. No, they were not cafeterias; they offered things on the cafeteria system: jobs, counseling, artistic training. Jobs. Weren't people going to have *jobs* anymore? Did Max say that? She was ill at ease. And that business of touching my neck, she thought, wasn't that a little pushy, after all, and what did he mean about giving me money to educate my children? She looked across the room. Victoria was standing next to a good-looking young man. *Don't the*

young people look sweet together, she thought. But of
course they won't have children (she thought). No one
has children. *I* don't have children. *What did he mean
about giving me money to send my children to college?*

Max went on. He talked about crime and surplus people.
He proposed a system of *deferred sustained maintenance*
for well-meaning surplus people. For others, he said with
regret, he could only propose (and here was a point on
which he and the President were in agreement) a system
of *incapacitation.*

Incapacitation. Sophie looked up. Had she been dozing?
She never dozed. She was very severe about people dozing.
Still, she didn't remember exactly what had gone before,
just looking at Victoria and drifting off and then this new
word *incapacitation* again. She returned to herself. Spuyterkill (National Conservators' Council — open to the public) stiffened her backbone. Land View (Carmelite Sisters,
on the market) put sparkle in her eye. No. 220 Fifth
Avenue (demolished) gave her voice. "Max," she said
sternly. "Naturally, some of us know all about *incapacitation,* and exactly what it is, but others, I feel, do not.
Definition, please," and she leaned forward attent (she was
determined not to doze) and a little disapproving.

"It's very simple, Sophie, as you know," Max said. "It
involves identifying those criminals who are utterly com-
mitted to a criminal life-style and keeping them in prison,
which is to say, away from the rest of us, for life."

"Or until they are rehabilitated," Sophie said securely,
adding a footnote.

"I'm afraid that's a little naive, Sophie," Max said.

Sophie looked at him. There was a pause. *In my own
house,* she thought.

"I believe in rehabilitation," she said. She did. She believed in it in the way she believed in certain stores for linen. She was sure she believed in it. And in her heart she was sure she was going to be told now that it was going out of business. It did happen. Things went out of business. The inheritance went to different corners of the room. Land View (Carmelite Sisters — on the market) went to stand by Van Aspair, who was fiddling with the button on his jacket. No. 220 Fifth Avenue (demolished) curled into the smoke of the cigarette in the hand of Biki Post. Spuyterkill (National Conservators' Council — open to the public) disappeared behind Victoria Feldman. *I wonder is anything wrong with her?* Sophie thought, looking at Victoria.

Then the young man next to Victoria spoke. "How can you divorce wealth from work?" he asked.

Max said: "It has already happened, I'm afraid, but it has not yet been accepted."

"But work, striving, is the process we are meant to be in; wealth is only the overt reward that keeps people in the process."

Max smiled. "So it would be better to ask people to work without promising them any reward than to give them a reward promising them no work?" he asked, engagingly, knowing the power of rewards.

"Exactly," the young man said. "Work is instruction and allows for the formation of natural authority."

"Oh yes?" Max asked. The idea was new.

"If a pipe leaks and a man says, 'Hand me that tool,' and another man hands it to him and the leak is then fixed, the fixer assumes, in the course of his action, a natural authority over the event, and both men learn from the event and are drawn close within the event."

"What if the second man resents the first man for knowing how to fix the leak?"

"He will not; not if he wants the leak fixed."

"What if the first man lords it over the second man as he shows his superior skill?"

"He will not, if he is concentrating on his work."

"And you will be able to persuade your two friends to work without prospect of wealth?"

"To work without *thinking about* wealth; yes, they will be willing to do that."

Among the wraiths in the room there was some confusion. The older Aspairs could not be persuaded to oppose the idea of work (the first Johannes was fixed in his opinion that it was necessary), but later members of the family (especially the imperial Mrs. James-James II) refused to give up the idea of thinking about wealth, which, they said, provided them more comfort and delight than the mere possession of wealth ever did. Among the inheritors there was suspicion and doubt. Asked to express an opinion about the impending divorce of work and wealth and which side would they take, the Carmelite Sisters said that they deplored divorce in all instances and would not say more, and they did not say more, not at least until the Conservators, a somewhat bolder group, issued a communiqué saying that while work in the form of *fine craftsmanship* was certainly desirable, it could hardly be expected to long survive in the current climate without a large endowment. Upon hearing the word *endowment*, the Carmelite Sisters, afraid that they had missed a funding opportunity, began to speak all at once about the conditions prevalent at Land View, which, according to them, were very dire. They mentioned falling cornices, chipping plaster, ruptured plumbing (which made for them, they said, the example of the leaking pipe, chosen by the young man, especially poignant, as they had not, so far, been able to afford the services of a good plumber, and did he really know one who would be willing to work for nothing, because in their experience, plumbers were very high-priced articles indeed). They mentioned also: heaving parquet, clogged gutters, broken slate (here they said they were forced to agree with the Conservators that only a huge endowment could ever hope to cover the expenses involved in keeping up a slate roof), and slippery steps. They retired a little fatigued, feeling as usual that they had not really been listened to, pining as always for a certain small cottage in California that would better suit their reduced number (the Sisters were down to four) and their modest purse.

Sophie was distressed. Here at last was real talk, and yet she was not happy. She had begun to focus on the question of rehabilitation versus incapacitation when, rather rudely, she thought, her attention had been taken somewhere else. Real talk, she felt, would not carom around like this. Perhaps this wasn't real talk. Perhaps she should *stop it.*

The young man talked on and on. Max, she noticed, seemed unable to stop him. Max said yes, but that the two fellows fixing the leak lived in a microcosm, and the young man said that that's where all people did live, in a microcosm. Max said (easy laugh) that the young man seemed to be a *metaphysician,* not an economist, and the young man said *exactly,* as though now they were in agreement and could begin the real talk.

Real talk. Sophie was besieged with choices. She hated choices. Above all in life, she liked simplicity. She wanted to know when to get into the multiservice concept and when to get out. She had just begun to work on that difficult issue when she was asked to make other decisions, more difficult still, about work and wealth, the macrocosm and the microcosm. *Too much,* Sophie thought, but she felt unable to act, for around her, enclosing these other questions like a fog, was the crucial question to which she had as yet no answer: *Was this real talk or not?*

People were uneasy, waiting for a decision. Van Aspair felt that soon he would be called on to say something. Metaphysics, he thought. The Cave. *But what was in it?*

Nina thought: That boy has crashed.

Victoria thought: I wonder if he has noticed me.

Sophie looked and looked. She searched the room for clues. The boy talked on and on. The room had parted, in a way. Max had retreated. He spoke only from time to time, offering small modifications. The young man took to asking Max for a response, leaving openings, urging him along. He spoke at length about corporate fascism and asked Max if he didn't agree that in a situation in which work and wealth were divorced, and wealth was entirely an indirect benefit, meted out by a central authority, that fascism would be the result in the end, or even, in fact, the proper name for the thing at the beginning. Max said only that *fascism* was a tricky word and that many people used it incorrectly.

Then the voice of the Aspairs was heard. It enclosed the fish and the furs of the Columbia River; enclosed the vast rents derived from the speculative housing erected upon the Cozfen Farm; enclosed the Prophets' Dances (the

123

most exclusive of subscription events) and the famous
Electric Light Ball given by Mrs. James-James II, at which
the sheep were finally demarked from the goats. It enclosed the Carmelite Sisters and the National Suicide Prevention Bureau; it enclosed the barnacles on the sweet
young body of Johannes Aspair IV and the corrupt flesh
of the demented Cuyler Aspair (never mentioned) and
the almost beatific gaze of the saintly Alice-Marie Aspair,
who had found her work among the poor and among *poets*
and *artists*. The voice of the Richest Man in America was
clearly heard. At home, rising from history and from
the authority of history, it swept through the rooms of
the last Mrs. Aspair. But it wasn't Sophie talking, it was
Biki Post.

"I don't see what was so bad about Mussolini. He was
always damned nice to me," she said.

The room changed. What had parted met again. Sophie
rose up into certainty. If Biki Post was in it, it wasn't real
talk after all. Van Aspair settled into his chair. The young
man stood crushed. And all this time, Sophie saw, another
process had been at work right under her nose. During the
confusion, even as her rooms had been swathed in fog
(leaving her for the first time in years within an atmosphere of *doubt*), another process, benign, reliable, and
her own, had been at work. Sophie thought: within this
deferred sustained maintenance, why not *a multiservice
approach?* She looked up. Her room made sense. All but —
who was he?

"I wonder if you could tell me," she said, sweet as pie,
"exactly who you are?"

The young man blushed.

Van Aspair thought: *I don't know him.*

Nina thought: oh, dear.

Victoria said, "Sorry, darling, not to tell. He's Timothy Furlong, friend of mine. Came to pick me up." There was an uncertain quiet. Victoria looked for, found, and then spent her last bit of assurance. It was pieced out of some days she had spent with her father; happy times playing all-girl sports at Saint Cecilia's School in Josephtown, Maryland, and good things she remembered that had happened at parties. "We're going dancing," she said.

There was quiet. Sophie thought: that girl is in some sort of trouble. Then she thought: they're not going dancing. Then she thought: *all of you go home.*

The party dispersed.

Quickly, Victoria left with Timothy Furlong. That was his name. She knew it perfectly well. She remembered from dances: Junior Gaiety, Middle Gaiety, Senior Gaiety. My dear, think of it, she thought. Some good comes of these things.

Sophie, alone in her rooms with Max, felt a new assurance. Max, newly grateful, curled at her feet. There was no distance between them. He understood exactly: *multiservice within the context of deferred sustained maintenance.* Sophie spoke her mind. "You know, Max," she said, "I have always seen myself as occupying a role set apart from politics. I see now that I have been mistaken. I am — going, going — foolish, a woman, *foolish!*"

Max, seated at her feet, allowed his head to drift over to her leg. "I think I will have the President to dinner," Sophie said. To herself, she added (thinking of the old

arrangement — family, the world of work, the open mind):
but not with that crew.

On the street, the young man introduced himself to
Victoria. It wasn't Timothy Furlong after all. His name
was William Guin.

"Can I give you my number?" Victoria asked.

"Oh yes," William Guin said. "Thank you very much."

On the street, Biki Post stood talking to Nina. Nina
stood close to the curb, waving for a taxi. Biki talked and
talked. She said it was absolutely true what people said
about Frank Post cheating at cards, and she recited again
the old story about how she got her black eye, and she said
that Frank Post had hardly ever caught any sailfish at all,
and that if the world knew, all those trophies belonged to
Alfredo, the captain. Nina was patient. She was a patient
woman. She was a kind woman. Still, it *was trying.* When
she began the "Nina Knows" column, she had sworn: *no
lies.* And she didn't lie. She went into a certain group and
told the truth. Then there was a change. She didn't have
to lie, exactly, but she did have to make up the group. She
went into rooms where there was one familar face and then
just caterers and people from the sucker lists and she went
home and wrote: *Mona Davis in her fabulous emeralds
and others too chic to mention.* She had done it for years:
Lizzie Hannah, Nin-Nin Shaw; you know, like that. Like
what? She was not sure that she knew. A taxi came and she
disengaged herself from Biki Post. She wanted to say something to comfort Biki, who looked very sad, but Biki, she
knew, wouldn't get the point, so she said: "I'll do what I
can, darling, but people don't follow Frank much any-

more," and she got into the cab. On the way home, she thought about her evening. *Next year Sophie will have Miss Quality and I can go home to Georgia,* she thought. She was from Georgia. Her father was still there. He owned land and a chain of drugstores. She had a family and plenty of money. She didn't have a worry in the world. "Miss Quality," she said out loud, "or that man from the *National Puzzler.*"

---❉{ 7 }❉---

THE HOTEL HERVER

NIGHT fell. Esther was more and more alone. One by one the other individuals in the room lost substantiality. She looked up and they were gone. Wraiths took their place. Her mother arrived with nourishing food (which Esther rejected cruelly), then went to sit just out of view in the shadows, watching patiently. Something wanted? Are you cool? Are you warm? Esther moved her chair so her back was against the dark.

Miss Henry came and sat on the edge of her desk. Jaunty, slim, a little cruel-looking, she was dressed in a trim grey suit; she wore a hat. She smoked cigarettes, one after the other; Esther's brand.

> Miss Henry has become by the death of her grandfather the richest two-year-old child in the world.

It was the best story Esther knew; she wished she could print it in her column. Unfortunately, it was more like something from "Nina Knows" than anything else. How she longed to know Nina! Sometimes, when she least expected it, she looked around her in some room and saw Nina. At these moments she felt an almost irresistible impulse to run up to her and ask her forgiveness (she was cutting into Nina's circulation); she imagined that Nina would stroke her head gently (somehow, she felt, her head would be *bowed*) and that everything would be all right between them. But how this could ever really happen in fact, she did not know, since she had an idea, equally strong, that she must *continue* to cut into Nina's circulation.

Esther got up and pushed her chair back with her legs. She listened to the sound of it scraping along the floor. Suddenly she had a picture of herself in the room. She saw the whole room with herself in it, pushing the chair back from her desk. She saw it from above; it was receding; receding.

She went to see McFaran. McFaran was one of the Canadians. His title was vague; the Canadians seemed to rotate titles. They were everywhere and nowhere. They were everything and nothing.

McFaran was the Canadian for her, at any rate. She never saw another one to talk to. Whenever she needed a Canadian, he was there, waiting.

Their meetings were usually short. She would go to his office, where he would be sitting alone with no work around him, as though he existed only for her. He would smile; he would read her copy, quickly.

He read so quickly; it was as if he only needed to touch the paper to understand it. "Good; good; don't get this, this word here," he would say pointing to a word; but even as he stopped to show her what he meant, it was as though he kept right on reading. "Oh yes? New on the streets?" he would say, hardly looking at the paper, looking more at *her*, questioning something he was reading in *her*. "Very well then. Ha. Ha. That's nice. Thank you, Esther. Phone in more later? Something bright? Good. Good. Ta-Ta."

He actually did say "Ta-Ta." It was what unnerved her more than anything, even more than the bad way in which he unashamedly dressed. *Ta-Ta*. Was it something they said in Canada? Did it make fun of something they said in Canada? Was it something they said in Canada to make fun of the kind of thing she aspired to in the United States? It was one of the phrases in the language about which she could form no point of view.

He was waiting for her. He read her copy, approved it, then showed her something from the morning tabloid, a story from California. A young boy had killed his girl friend and then told all his friends. His friends went up one by one to the ravine where her body was to see if she was dead. One poked at her with a stick. Miss Quality winced. She did not like to work on stories from out of town.

"Did this *slip by?*" McFaran asked, smiling.

"Out of *town*," Esther said.

"We did *think* about it?"

"Oh yes: 'Peek-a-Boo Boys.'"

McFaran laughed, and in a slightly different way than he had ever laughed before: letting her in on it more. *Another test*, Esther thought.

"Oh, I like that." McFaran said. "Do I see it right — echo of the kind of *blouse?*"

She nodded and took a look at him. McFaran laughed again. By the end of this laugh, he had come back to an ambiguous tone. "Too bad we missed using *that*; but out-of-town; I understand exactly," he said.

The Richest Tot In The World

Miss Henry (above) has become by the death of her grandfather the richest two-year-old child in the world. The tiny heiress to the Henry Stores fortune is seen here with her nurse. (Globe News Photo—watch your credit)

Thought Esther, reentering the city room. Miss Henry? Miss Henry was gone. The desk she had sat on was flat and empty. Esther avoided it and passed out into the hall. She rang for the elevator. The sound of the bell could be heard throughout the building. She heard doors slam and the whir of a motor. After a time, a small boy with thin cheeks and bulging eyes opened the door at her floor and she stepped into the elevator. Did she leave her mother behind? Deep in the dark room, her mother rose up in fright. She did not mind being alone. She was always alone. She wondered about the *cold. Will you be all right with just that little jacket?* Esther put her hands over her ears. The elevator arrived at the lobby.

On the street there was a little rain, almost a mist. *So like the moisture your skin had in youth,* Esther thought. *The suppleness; women the world over have known the secret for years; now, in America, skins over thirty-five . . .* The mist fell on her skin. She felt her skin blush under it. She blushed under all touches. Touched by a man, she *jumped.*

She sighed. She was under obligation. She was required to visit her friend Galen. She had abandoned her mother, but she would not abandon him. Abandon him? The thought did not occur to her; that is, it did occur to her, more and more often, but she rejected it. She still rejected it, but more and more feebly.

She was required to visit Galen every night. She envisioned the group that would be there around him: small Lucy; fat Germanic Karen with her hair in a coil around her head. They were like opera characters. That was, indeed, where they had met — at the opera. Out of all the *fans*, the *fanatics* for opera who occupied the Standing Room, this small group had emerged. She had learned things from this: how a group emerged from a larger group; how within even a very small group there were shades and distinctions; how, very often, it was the decisive act of one person that determined the sphere within which a group would operate; finally, how it was necessary, really very necessary (if the group was to continue to exist) that the history of this decisive act be told and told again. *Jerome, he take out shib, cut Silky,* she thought. Her friend Galen was like a dead rabbit: round and white. He was repulsive in some ways.

So like the fluids your skin had in youth, she thought.

Walking along the street, she was not happy. The light rain touched her face. It was making her skin a little raw. The light drops that had so far merely rested on the surface of her fine worsted jacket would in time penetrate.

I won't go, she thought. It was true; something to be faced; she had outgrown them. She had never liked the others, not ever, but Galen had so spread his charm over them all that it was possible to ignore . . . what? Suddenly, cruelly, she felt as though she must honestly catalog the faults of her friends: the *self-delusion*, first of all; they talked as though they lived among titans or poets, but they lived, in fact, with their families — except for Galen, that is, who lived in two tenement rooms and made a family

out of *them*. She stopped in weariness and in self-disgust.
These were, after all, her friends. They had pushed her
ahead, after all; they had encouraged her to leave her
mother — although they stayed with their own; they followed with selfless curiosity all her progress through a world
into which they themselves would never enter; at times
they had even made one or two *suggestions*.

Not they; Galen only. If it hadn't been for Galen, she
would have left the little group long ago. But he had been
her friend, and something more — her mentor. When she
told him what she thought she might do at the paper, he
said: "Tell them you are a new kind of sob sister: you don't
cry." She had told them that. And later, after she had begun the column (it was not then a column, actually, but
only a series of crime paragraphs set off in a box), he said:
"Say more about the clothes"; and it was this idea, put into
practice, that had set her off from other writers about
violence and given her her first success. She thought about
this, and then she thought about his drinking and his
puffiness and his dirtiness. Nevertheless, she decided that
she would stop after all, and then she thought: *Forget
about it; you can see him tomorrow night.*

Esther stopped at the Subway Club. She hated the Subway Club and wanted, in her heart, to destroy it. It was
filled with drug users and drug dealers and the worst
Europeans, but it was easy to pick up a "bright" item here.

She had her own table. On some nights one of the bright
humorists she admired would come and sit. Otherwise it
was more purposeful and businesslike and she went home
feeling that she had been drained of something.

What are you doing, *sportswear?*

She said this to a European. It was her conceit that all Europeans aspired to have their own line of sportswear.

She spoke in kind of a growl when she was at the Subway Club; she puffed on the toughest brand of non-filtered cigarettes. She was rude. She sipped on a special nonalcoholic cocktail with fruit ("my Shirley Temple," she called it) and sucked on the cherry. Often, when approached at her table, she didn't ask the person to sit down. The person *stood*, whether prince, count, pimp, or dealer.

Once or twice she had been *used*. She quoted the picturesque speech of certain dealers and later found out that the special expressions they used ("O-Kee, Doe-Kee"; "Slats Mor-Atts") were the brand names of the heroin they sold. She banished these particular dealers from her column. Was that good enough?

Nina wouldn't touch it with a ten-foot pole.

She went to see Galen. She was surprised to find him alone. Suddenly, the group was reduced to its essential elements. His eyes were open wide. Continue? they asked. Or not.

He was sitting on a dirty velvet sofa. Once, he had said that he thought it had "good lines"; it didn't; he didn't think so. It was his, nonetheless, and it was velvet. From a *distance*, from the highest and most remote circle, it might be perceived as having good lines.

This is what he meant: the others see me as though from the highest and most remote circle. You see me close up. What do you see?

She did see him. His face was like the face of a dying animal; it shone in just that way; great wisdom, but dumb wisdom, and dying; ineffectual. His body was white and puffy; she could not keep her mind from Silky, the rabbit killed by Jerome. Galen was not clean. He was like a rabbit in a dirty box.

Incongruously, she thought: *he is not helping me.* All at once she understood that this was a real issue. At all times he threw up his charm between other persons and the fact of his degenerate condition. Now, he would not do it. *See me?* She turned away.

Now it's settled, she thought, and she almost got up. But she was held in place. It was *sound* that held her. It was his voice. He was beginning to sing. His voice was thin and high.

> *She huddles for warmth*
> *Just under the awning*
> *What a downpour it is —*
> *Her escort is yawning,*

"Miss Henry at the track," Galen said.

She looked. All his charm was back. It was possible to look at him and not see him. He sang on.

> *In anticipation of further delays,*
> *They've been waiting and waiting*
> *For days and for days,*
> *But Miss Henry won't* budge —
> *She stays and she stays . . .*

Miss Henry at the track. He was reminding her that their friend Miss Henry belonged as much to him as to herself; that to leave him was to leave part of *her*; he was saying this, and saying also that he submitted to her opinion of him.

135

But her opinion had changed again. She felt a disgust that he could not possibly submit to. She left.

She went home — to the Hotel Herver. The door flew open; no agency of human hands.

She was small in the lobby. In the lobby, she looked like a receptacle.

No one was about. The lights were yellow. The management, agents of a partial renovation, had sought to introduce a *glow*. Better blue, she thought, thinking of supermarkets.

She sat in a chair. All alone. She looked up. Small screens were there, eight of them, showing dots arranged into: hallways, doorways, the roof. *Me too?* she wondered. She pushed herself along the floor in her chair, angling herself into view. *Yes, yes*, she thought, seeing on screens: dots arranged into hallways, doorways, *herself*, the roof. *Media pressure*, she thought.

She was a thoughtful person. That was why she had had to leave home. Now, looking at the screens, her thoughts turned to *bellboys*, and it occurred to her that the tiny dots on the closed-circuit video screens were *like* bellboys running back and forth between some job (hallways, doorways, the roof) and a bell-desk (the screens); forever on the job and at the bell-desk both; forever in transit, too, from one place to the other. But this made her remember that there weren't any bellboys, in fact, to run fetch her a pack of cigarettes (she wanted a smoke), and she began to be almost sad.

Perhaps she was sad already. She put her eyes on the screens. She put aside the meaning of the configurations the dots were arranged into and looked at the dots one by one. These bellboys (the dots) didn't seem to belong to the *decor* — the way real bellboys did, who certainly would wear a bit of braid, for instance — but rather to the street, which they seemed to let in, not protect against.

She stood up. Then she walked right up to the screens. Everything seemed blue and grey on them. There was no movement, just long stretches of unbroken time. Miss Quality thought: phone something in; something *bright*. Then she went up to bed.

-⊶⊰ *Three* ⊱⊷-

THE PEARL BUTTON GANG

8

BAD NEWS

THE telephone rang at a few minutes before nine o'clock. Edward Jones was in his bed. His friends were under instruction not to ring before ten. From his bed he thought: no. The courtesy of his friends was such that they honored his injunction in all circumstances. A call of emergency came at ten o'clock, and a minute or two for additional courtesy. There was another sort of call, of course, much beyond emergency, and that sort of call might come at any time; but that call had an aspect of fright. This call was merely insistent.

He did not go back to sleep. Instead, he had this thought: A boy of fourteen killed his girl friend and threw her into a ditch. Later his friends came by. One kicked the dead girl to see if she was still alive. Later, another friend came by. He threw a stone on her to see if she was still alive.

Then he thought: Alice Hamilton had fourteen identical Rolls-Royces.

The telephone rang again. He put it out of his mind. It is the same person, he thought.

The telephone rang again shortly after ten o'clock. Edward Jones (dressed, refreshed, looking healthy and shiny) picked it up. It was his friend Lila. It was his privilege to have her first call of the day.

"Hello, darling," he said.

"Hello, Eddy. Are you terribly comfortable?"

"Very comfortable," he said.

They discussed events. They discussed various social events of the night before that neither had attended. This was a matter of habit. Sometimes they did it quickly, for the record; at other times they were longer at it.

"Mrs. Freddy Beech. I see Mrs. Freddy Beech," Lila said, "bobbing for the chin of Mr. Freddy Beech as for a small apple."

"And *speaking*," Eddy said. "Putting word after word. That is the wonder of Mrs. Freddy Beech."

Then they talked of other news. Lila very quickly gave hers, which was news of what her doctors had said. Eddy reported something of what had gone on in the world according to the newspapers.

"In California," he said, "a fourteen-year-old boy killed his girl friend and threw her into a ditch. Various friends of his were sent by him to look at her, dead."

"What a story, Eddy."

"I haven't been able to think about anything else."

"Not chivalrous."

"Not chivalrous."

"How do you think she looked to them?"

"*Abstract*, I think."

"I have never liked anything abstract. Never."

"I know."

"Which is why I like clothes so much, I think. Clothes are so specific."

"Yes."

"Have you seen any pretty clothes, Eddy? Tell me what you've seen."

And then they talked about clothes.

Most of the men and women in Edward Jones's life did not try to fathom him. People he knew (most people he knew) moved in the same direction, always; often were dizzy; and rarely had time to think. Their movement was toward advantage. Eddy saw movement differently: moving toward pleasure, perhaps. He did not want to talk about what he saw, though, and this was why a life in the world of fashion suited him: the boundaries of the fashionable world he knew enclosed pleasure, but the talk was of advantage, always.

There were other men in New York with whom he might have been confused: men who were alone except when they were in the company of public women. But there was no confusion. Nanno de Huerd, Sandy Ebberstael, Belin Forst were remarked on. They were named. *Nin-Nin Shaw, in Galanos with Nanno de Huerd.* Eddy saw Nin-Nin Shaw, but his name was not publicly linked with hers or with anyone's. He stepped aside, discreetly. *But of course they want you, Nin-Nin.* It was not difficult to do. It was like a reverse in waltzing. Eddy was a good dancer. He waltzed without effort (not that there was any longer a chance to waltz). *They do not reverse,* Eddy sometimes thought as he saw a person circle around into dizziness.

He looked after himself carefully. He took good care of

his person and his house and his clothes. He did not do any laundry or cleaning, of course, but he brushed his own hats and he polished his own shoes. As for his shoes, they were mostly brown. On them he put a coat of brown polish, buffed them, then applied, lightly, a coat of black. He spent one morning a week with his shoes. He spent every morning at home. His rooms were two rooms on the third floor of a limestone house in East Seventy-third Street. No one was ever asked to his rooms. He had tea in the afternoon, his mother's set, in the front room, a chair set within a bay window, angled to provide a view west. After seven o'clock in the evening, he was likely to be out.

Eddy was small. His body was slightly rounded, like a stone under water. He was not weak, however. There were times when people were startled; if an elevator failed, he could carry something quite heavy up many flights of stairs.

His head was large, rather too large for his body, and it was heavy-looking. He had a square chin; he had under his eyes the deep depressions that ministers sometimes have, or serious businessmen. His eyes were heavy, dark, and sad.

Edward Coonlon Jones was more than sixty years old. His friendship with Lila Prain-Codman-Aspair-Yormin (by friends always called Lila Codman) had gone on for more than fifty years. Everything about him was old, but it was fresh.

The light in his front room was fresh, but it was not direct light. In morning at this season sunlight barely hit the panes of glass in the windows; but there was light enough.

The room was divided in two by light. One half was lit softly, the other more softly still. Light came in through three windows in the bay. A silk prayer rug lay half in the bay and half out of it. A small Empire armchair was on the rug, faced toward the westernmost window of the bay, a small table beside it. Here Eddy sat for several hours each day, reading or watching or listening, or (between four-thirty and five in the afternoon) drinking tea.

The half of the room that was lit very softly was boundaried by the southern border of a Tabriz rug. This rug had a ground of dull pink upon which were figures of pale pink and ocher and other colors that always slipped a person's mind. Whether there was some green in the rug or anything actually red was hard to tell. In any case, the whole was well faded.

Eight of his mother's Adam-Sheraton chairs stood around the edges of the rug. They were not faded or dull. They gleamed. The green was obtrusive. They were not meek. The other four chairs, together with the painted desk, were in Eddy's bedroom, against a wall — one, two, three, four, five. His bedroom was large, but it seemed to be crowded by reason of the chairs, the desk, the large bedstead (the carved bed of his grandparents'), and a profusion of shelves, cabinets, and built-out closets that ran from floor to ceiling and contained: linen, silver, china, and clothes.

Things flowed to him. Dealers sought him out: *Mr. Jones, we have a particularly fine example of this or that, and knowing of your interest . . .* , they wrote. Friends gave him presents; people remembered him in their wills. Things flowed to him and would have engulfed him, except that he turned the stream away, gently. Given a thing, he found a chance to give it away again, and partly by reason of his generosity (and the high quality of his inventory), he received as many invitations to weddings, baptisms, birthday and anniversary celebrations as if he had been the head of a clan or a political club. Asked to take his pick, he took little. Asked to buy, he paid with a compliment. He kept to what he had. As for the future, he had arranged to give what he had to his friends. He had sorted it out piece by piece in small legacies. His worry was the chairs. He had left them to Lila originally, but now it seemed likely that he would outlive Lila. Lila had no successors; no one he could find. A *museum*, he thought. *Imagine*. He put the decision off.

So, it seemed that he was ordered and balanced in his regard for possessions. In a way this was so, but the balance was not entirely within this one set of rooms. The rooms in which Eddy sat and slept and watched were not the whole scale, but only one arm of it. Against them was weighed another set of rooms, equal in extent, on the floor above, in which were stored: clothes. When Eddy lay down at night, they rested on his head. He had in his owner-ship the suits and hats and shoes of Michael Coonlon; the suits, hats, and shoes of Robert C. Prain; some examples from the wardrobes of Howard Prain, Louise Van Rens-selaer Prain, Alida Van Horne Van Rensselaer, and Miss Margaret Dana. He had a very large collection of the hats, shoes, gloves, coats, dresses, suits, and opera cloaks of Sarah Coonlon Jones. He had clothes that had belonged to many other persons as well. There were dresses by Worth and Pacquin and Callot Soeurs. There were ex-amples of Poiret. There were suits from Anderson & Shepard and James Bell. But it was by owner and not by maker that the clothes were arranged. At the death of a friend, Eddy thought: *the closets*. Here was his mania. He did not fight against it much.

When Eddy and Lila had finished their talk, Eddy put down the telephone and, immediately, it rang again. He picked it up. It was his cousin Nanno de Huerd, the son of Rita de Herence and the Count of no account, as Michael Coonlon had named him. Nanno was not a welcome caller.

Often, Nanno called to bring bad news. There was a great deal of bad news in Nanno's own life — so much that he had long ago ceased to think of good news as a possibility for himself. Talk with Nanno was within the framework of bad news even when he had nothing to say. But often he did have something ugly to remark on in particular.

Now he mentioned a friend of Eddy's, a man called Henry Fourt. Henry Fourt was the sort of person Nanno disliked. Henry Fourt had a friend of long standing (a woman named Lizzie Hannah) and he did not tell gossip or complain. Nanno would have put up with him if he complained more.

"I don't know why he's so pleased with himself," Nanno said once. At other times he talked about Henry's friend Lizzie Hannah. He said:

"I don't think she gives him much money." And:

"I always like to have more than one string to my bow, but if that's what he likes, fine." And:

"I wouldn't put up with her for a minute." And:

"I never could stand a Jewess."

Eddy would have found all this easy to ignore except that he also had an impression that it would be hard to get along with Lizzie Hannah, and that despite her hard-bitten way of talking, she was not strong, but very changeable; and he sometimes detected signs of strain and unhappiness in his friend Henry; so that Nanno's statements were unwelcome echoes of his own thoughts, in part. Nanno (who knew that much of his best bad news glanced off his cousin without leaving any mark) multiplied his remarks on the subject for this reason.

"I've been calling you all morning," Nanno said in urgent, happy tones. "Lizzie is going to drop Henry Fourt; sell him off."

Nanno reported it that way: news of the market.

It was, in a way, news from the market. Elizabeth Hannah was the only daughter and favorite child of Jacob Verdel, an investment banker. Jacob Verdel, a master of the market, was the last millionaire to build a house in Fifth Avenue. Even at the time, the gesture seemed futile: other houses were already coming down. The house was built to echo the architecture of the Italian Renaissance in Florence, and it was filled with fine works of art, including a famous picture by Goya, which had descended, with many other objects, to Elizabeth Hannah. Elizabeth Hannah did not live in the Fifth Avenue house, of course, but rather in a large apartment in Park Avenue. Here, with her possessions (all rising in the market), she held court, in a way, with Eddy's friend Henry as a permanent guest. Henry Fourt — poor, and of impractical nature — preserved into early old age the attitudes of a student (he had been trained as an architect, but did not practice). Lizzie Hannah liked him because he knew all about her possessions. He was one of her possessions, in her view; and not the least one, either, since he was in some ways the key to all the others. Of course, he didn't come near to the Goya in her regard. She needed no help in appreciating the Goya.

"Why would Lizzie do that?" Eddy asked.

"It's Maureen. She's afraid Aunt Lizzie will leave him

some money." At times, Nanno, who was often prolix, dramatic, and vague, could come to the point.

How unfair, Eddy thought. When Nanno asked to meet him for lunch, he agreed to go.

They met at La Primavera, a fashionable restaurant made out of a butcher's shop. The masters of the decor had left all the old hooks (because they looked so strong) and all the strong white tile (because you can't get that quality anymore), but it was not entirely brutal: there were fresh flowers at each table.

Eddy arrived before Nanno did. He sat alone at a small table, with a bouquet of fresh flowers in front of him. He had time to contemplate the idea of talking with Nanno. There would be a great deal of disorganized talk, and some well-focused complaint. Complaint was the backbone upon which bloated self-concern was overlaid in Nanno's conversation. Only his overt complaint had integrity. He was at his best when he discussed tailors who did not take the proper care with his clothes or a taxi driver who had let him out too far from the curb; at least he spoke with conviction. He was at his worst when he decided to indulge his *exhaustion*. He had once told Eddy a story that, in Eddy's opinion, explained his fascination with his own capacity for tiredness. Once, Nanno said, he had played a trick on the employees of the Hotel Quirinale in Rome. "I told them that my family had gone off; that I was a little bit afraid. They gave me treats all day in consequence," Nanno said.

After a time, Nanno arrived. He was tall, thin, and febrile. He looked like an overgrown child with rickets. His clothes were luxurious (he wore a double-breasted suit; the lapels of the jacket had an exaggerated width and overpowered his small chest) and he wore jewelry; but there are poor people, too, who wear expensive clothes and who hold to the possession of a ring or bracelet even when they are hungry. The word that described Nanno was *undernourished.*

Nanno sat down. "I'm going to order salmon," Nanno said. "I won't talk to you if you don't have it too." This was the end of normal conversation. Without apology he collapsed into his chair and began a fit of wheezing that caused his head to move up and down in a violent way, so that at one moment his forehead (upon which a few strands of hair from another part of his head had been affixed) seemed about to hit the table, while, at the next, it rose up high. His head came to rest in this latter position — forehead up — and Nanno held it there. He seemed to be in a kind of artistic repose, from which no event in the world could possibly shake him; and Eddy, if he hadn't known that Nanno was incapable of sustained effort, might have supposed that his cousin would spend the whole of their time together looking at the ceiling.

"Who's that?" Nanno asked, turning his head around. "Over there."

Eddy looked. He saw a small, dark-haired girl dressed half in riding clothes, sitting with a man in an ugly brown suit.

"I don't know them," Eddy said.

"I know her from somewhere," Nanno said. "But look, he has a gun. Isn't that interesting?"

Eddy looked. There was a bulge in the man's jacket at the waist. "Oh, is that a gun do you suppose?" Eddy said.

"I'm going to get a gun, too," Nanno said. And then he got up and went to the lounge.

He was gone only a short time, and when he returned he was very bright. Without preamble, he began to talk very rapidly, and Eddy saw that he was expected to ignore all that had gone before and to enter into a new phase. This he was willing to do, but it took some cleverness since the phase Nanno was in now had been spun from a conversation, well under way, of which Eddy had no idea. *Began it in the bathroom,* Eddy guessed, and in this he was correct. Nanno, standing in front of a mirror, had looked down at a small roll of aluminum foil and decided that the ration of cocaine that he had allotted to this interval out of the house was not in any case sufficient for the time (suddenly interminable) that stretched before him. He decided, therefore, to use all of it immediately. I must get more, he thought. I might as well use all of this now since I must get more anyway. So he took all he had, which made him very bright, and since he had the sensible habit of not wasting any of those moments when he felt bright, he began the talk he meant to have with Eddy right away. He began it as a rehearsal, but the talk had a momentum of its own and it was hard to stop it. And he was doing so well he wasn't sure he *wanted* to stop it. By the time he reappeared at the table, he had taken several brilliant moves through his subject. He had introduced the topic in a most amusing way — not too lighthearted, just the right weight, edged with amusement, but not lacking in significance. And he had placed, with good discretion, into his text, a small hint of what he wanted Eddy to do for him, but he had done it with such tact that Eddy wouldn't mind at all. It had been done with skill, and it was spontaneous, above all; it was natural and uncontrived. Unfortunately, this brilliant part of the conversation was mostly over, and much of Nanno's brightness gone away with it by the time he arrived at the table, so that what Eddy heard were scattered remarks on the subject of a woman who was presented as an important person, but also as a clownish person whom intelligent people must shun.

"I am very pleased with her!" Nanno said. "I took her to Le Rennie and I must say she did very well. 'Don't talk to the waiter, darling, I'll do that,' I said, and do you know she didn't say a word. I believe Anton thought she was deaf and dumb! I laughed and laughed. She didn't say a word. I ordered in French, of course, and that had its effect, and, of course, Anton always does me so well. You must come with me someday. My treat, *naturellement.* You'll see how well they do me. I knew him since he was a child, you know. He was just a *lift boy.* He doesn't forget that, thank God. No airs with *me.* He remembers Mama, you see, and what rooms we used to have. If he gets grand at all, I just say something like, 'Now, Anton, I was just trying to remember, when we were at the Majestic, what were those rooms called we used to take?' I know how to play him, you see; but he likes a laugh, just like me." Nanno paused and looked at Eddy. Eddy saw his eyes: blank eyes. It was not a comfortable moment. Eddy forgot for a moment what the conversation had been. Something almost like hatred passed across Nanno, but it went away. He continued:

"He likes a laugh, just like me. He must have had a laugh at her because he came up afterwards and said, 'Is she deaf and dumb?' Isn't that a laugh?"

It was quiet for a moment. There was quiet in the whole restaurant. Eddy looked up. His eyes were full of interest. Everyone was dumb. He felt that he might speak . . .

But before he could speak, to his surprise, Nanno began the same conversation all over again. He said:

"I have a new friend. I'm very pleased with her! She is coming across quite nicely. I'm going to put her across, make no mistake. She doesn't know anybody. Doesn't know any*thing*. I'm putting her on to everybody. We go everywhere. We are entirely inseparable. You should see her apartment. You'd hate it! She is a perfect pig in a way. It's all pink!" He giggled. Eddy, who knew some good shades of pink, said only:

"Well, she is lucky to have you, Nanno."

"Exactly! Exactly!"

Nanno grew very excited. Eddy saw that everything was sliding into excitement. He sought to restrain the excitement. He said: "Still, Nanno, you know you mustn't move too fast, or with too little regard for what the rest of her life might be."

Nanno grew more excited. His head moved up and down very violently, and some of the hair came unstuck from his head.

"Exactly! Don't you think I know *that?* How to *play* her?"

Eddy said nothing. Nanno suddenly saw himself alone.

"I don't see why you are so disapproving," he said. "I don't see why you always go out of your way to *hurt* me!" Nanno looked stricken. Eddy, who was relieved to see the mania broken, said:

"Dear Nanno, of course I'm terribly pleased. I'm sure she's a very good thing for you; how can you think I disapprove when it seems to have done you so much good. You know I think of that first."

Nanno moved quickly into deep feeling. If Eddy's palm

had been open, he might have placed his bony hand in it. Eddy's hand was not available, so he retreated a little. He composed himself. *Composed* was the posture Nanno now assumed to show that he had just finished being brave.

Eddy said: "What is this about Henry Fourt, Nanno?"

Nanno was still, and then, suddenly, he was very businesslike.

"Maureen Baker's been campaigning against him all summer. Lizzie spent a week with her in Connecticut and I guess she won her point then. Maureen's been crowing about it, too. I saw her two days ago at Dealer's and she said: 'He'll have to find a new meal ticket.' Those were her exact words."

Eddy looked a little shaken. Nanno saw an opening. He threw himself into it. "Which is why I called you," he said, sincerely. "I thought you ought to know." He felt new strength. "Because I try to look out for *your* interests . . ." He saw the opening close up in front of his eyes.

"And who is this woman you have met, your new friend?"

"She's called Davis."

"From . . . ?"

"Oklahoma."

"And you need . . ."

"Some money to take her around for a while."

"I will send you a check."

Nanno did not say *thank you*, but he did say *excuse me* in a tone that implied *thank you*. He rose from the table; then he went to speak to the captain.

Eddy watched. The captain looked like an athlete gone to fat. He had a barrel chest and his neck was very large. *Like my uncles*, Eddy thought. Nanno was speaking.

Nanno gestured. Nanno gave his fist into the captain's hand, then went quickly to the lounge. A *shebeen,* Eddy thought. He stayed perfectly still, as he did when he felt a commotion around him.

Then there was a commotion. A young woman, well dressed, got up from her table, approached the captain, and began to shout. She raised her arm. It may have been that what she raised was her fist only, but the captain struck it down as though it were dangerous.

The young woman was taken to the door by a man with slicked black hair. He took her over the threshold. He walked behind her. Together, the man and the young woman walked by the big windows at the front of the restaurant. Big and well proportioned, these windows had etched into them representations of lilies and tulips. The girl, once outside the door, put on a street face. This struck Eddy. The face, tilted up, bore an unconvincing dignity. Eddy thought, *He's twisting her arm.*

Alone on the street, Edward Jones looked at the street. The air hovered around him. A *little walk,* he thought. He looked at his shoes. This pair had toes with more of a point than was usual with him. He was trying them out. A little bit of *Broadway,* he thought. He smiled. Interesting now that Broadway was gone to echo, mildly, the extremes of Broadway. *The subway.* The archetype for his shoes had been seen there. He used to ride the subway to look at the clothes. It was not so instructive now as formerly. On the IRT in 1948 he saw a big Negro man wearing orange-red shoes that came to a point, in which had been inlaid a sunburst (full of points) of a lighter color still. At the shoemaker's, he thought of himself sitting quietly, a big Negro man across the way, legs stretched out, orange-red shoes coming to a point. The IRT, 1948. He said coolly: "Now, Mr. Andragezzo; this time I think we want a leather of a slightly lighter tone, with the suggestion, at the toe, of a *point*." Mr. Andragezzo did not question him. He respects my taste in shoes, Eddy thought.

The streets were, for him, hills and valleys, full of toeholds, detours, escarpments, vistas. A slippery spot was avoided; a good lookout aimed for. Within the sidewalks were pathways known to him, and marked on the facades of the buildings there were blazings, some of them very old and hard to see.

He felt the street through his shoes. The soles put on his shoes by Mr. Andragezzo were, per his instructions, very thin. He wanted to feel things with his feet. His shoes were formed around his feet perfectly (Mr. Andragezzo was a consummate craftsman), so that they were hardly felt. The thin soles allowed the paths within the sidewalks to be felt.

He was quiet and alert. He moved easily along and was confronted with no obstruction. This did not mean he was in isolation. Quite the contrary. He was in company with the other people who were on the paths: himself when young (or later on; or in recent days); certain other living people; and the dead. All these bowed or nodded and greeted him in a friendly way. "It's Edward Jones," the dead remarked. "Out on the street."

On occasion his path intersected one of the other private path systems within the street. A drunken man, on one of the private paths drunken men use, would look up and see Edward Jones. A man like this greeted Edward Jones politely now, and was greeted politely by him in return.

Such a man was on other old ways — was ancient himself, was resident in one of the old places (Hotel Rex; Hotel Prince), and was recognized by Eddy as belonging to the nobility of the city.

Eddy left the street and entered an art gallery. Here he looked at drawings of unbuilt buildings: of a National Cathedral (unbuilt); a National Library (unbuilt); a mint, a city hall, a Musical Archive (all unbuilt). He walked just behind a tall person who had on his face the smile of a boy and the remnant of a boy's bad complexion: his friend Henry Fourt. Several of the drawings in view had been done by Henry Fourt as a young man. Henry pointed them out, shyly.

"Who would have thought they ever would have seen the light of day?" Henry Fourt said.

"They are very fine," Eddy said.

"Imagine, the *Beaux Arts*," Henry said, moving on. "It's a wonderful surprise. But *here*." He stopped. The two men faced two views: different aspects of a plan for a National Musical Archive (unbuilt).

"Not to be sold — *see*," Henry said, pointing out a little green disk attached to the label on each. "One for you, dear Eddy. One for Lizzie."

"How is Lizzie?" Eddy asked, putting his head forward toward one view of a plan for a National Musical Archive, noticing the big dome, the big staircase splitting in two, an echo of Vienna.

"Perfectly fine."

"Here this winter?"

"We'll be off to Florida soon, I expect."

Eddy stood back from the Musical Archive. Looking around, he saw a girl. *Aspair*, his mind told him, sorting quickly, first result; Aspair-Feldman-Bolsorsky-Post — *Feldman*, final tally read. He bowed. "How is your money, Henry?" he asked.

"Oh, I haven't any," Henry Fourt said, laughing.

Edward Jones, walking home, thought: Now, Victoria Feldman, how old, my dear, over thirty, oh yes, over thirty for sure; thirty-five perhaps; perhaps more than *that*? Imagine. I wonder what her life is like. Not married. Never been married. A change from the mother. An improvement? In some ways. That *awful* Biki Post. Still, not so bad as . . .

Here he began to think about someone unpleasant. He felt it in his stride. Usually he walked with a steady gait that had been especially developed by him: it could take him over miles and miles without his thinking about it; but it did not obliterate the landscape in the way some people's walking did. He could stop in a second if something interesting came up. Now, all of a sudden, his stride was off.

Not so bad as Moo Moo Baker, he thought.

He walked on. He passed several badly dressed people. Why do people dress like that? he wondered.

Then, for fun, he ran it down: *Let's see. Johannes I, of course; Johannes II; then James-James II, married Ama Stone; then James-James III, and that's where I come in, come to think of it, old Gladys, meeting old Gladys, then who? Not Corneil, not James-James IV, but Petrus . . .*

Here he was coming back into the present, where, for some reason, he did not want to be, so he went back again and thought: *I wonder if any of the old property: in the Ninth Ward, for instance, or along Broadway. Now if Johannes II set up a trust for, let us say, one of his great-*

grandchildren (*certainly a possibility, since he lived so long*), *who would be, for instance: Corneil, Petrus, James-James IV, the young man who drowned, or Sixte, then that trust would still be alive, the third generation still being alive in the person of Victoria Feldman, for example.*

And this made him think about his connection to Victoria Feldman: *Grandaddy saw Johannes Aspair II, and Grandaddy and Mary Carmody saw Mrs. James-James II dressed up like an electric light. And I met Mrs. James-James III when she was an old lady, and everything after that is just part of daily life. We have known nearly all her people.* This made him begin to feel that he was responsible for her. *I wonder if she has any money?* he thought.

He thought about Victoria's mother and all her divorces. Then he thought about Henry Fourt's enemy Maureen Baker, whom people called Moo Moo, and who was the same sort of woman as Victoria's mother except more athletic. *Now I have to talk to Moo Moo*, he thought. *Soon.*

He walked. *New York City*, he thought. *Always something left.*

He entered the subway system and rode it two stops. He emerged and entered a bar. The Irish Echo, it was called.

"How are you today, Eddy?" the bartender said from behind the bar.

"Fine and dandy," Eddy said, taking a draft beer into his hand. Echo of Coonlon First.

--ᵈᵉ{ 9 }ᵉᵈ--

WILLIAM GUIN

WILLIAM GUIN had discovered that the city was essentially backward-looking; from a very early age he had ceased to believe in its future. He saw that the future-promoters were *priers*; with violent tools they pried apart some existing connection (roof to walls; floor to joists) so that they could squeeze themselves or other persons into position. This done, they turned backward and paid no attention to new thoughts.

He saw windows as resting on breathing torsos and roof elements as lying uneasily upon a course of human bodies. It was his opinion that solid matter would shrink from contact with flesh and not bond, and that the weakness in things would be seen first at some place where human flesh had been inserted and had failed to carry weight. The window was meant to rest on a beam, not a torso. The roof lay unsnugly on the bodies under it. But the prying-apart went on; soon a roof took two courses of humans instead of one; at each window opening, a human kneeled on the torso supporting the window and stretched his arms out to

160

the top of the opening, where another human was pulled like plastic around the top of the window, legs dangling down the other side.

It was like steerage — flesh piled on flesh — but when a voice was heard, it was always news of the *First Class* that it spoke of. One woman slept with her head tucked under the arm of another; the other protested; but there was nothing to be done. It was part of what life was like in the First Class.

How was he to think of himself? He took to the streets and was careful about what buildings he entered. Out on the street, he touched the stone under his feet, liking its solid feel. He touched the first joint of buildings, where a building met the street. His touch was very light; the cushion of his fingertips passed by and felt the small outcropping of granite or limestone on the surface of the wall of a building.

Where the joints were intact, he sometimes entered. What was he doing? His friend Arthur had forced him to admit that he no longer believed in democracy.

ARTHUR: You are looking for evidence of the integrity of labor.

WILLIAM: Yes.

ARTHUR: Among men and in buildings.

WILLIAM: Yes.

ARTHUR: But this is an aristocratic pursuit, since you ignore the work of the mass of men and even despise it. The *farmer,* the *craftsman,* the honest laborer, these are aristocratic figures, aren't they? — since they are free of the obligation, put on the mass of men, to work without satisfaction. And can the farmer, the craftsman, the laborer continue in their *untainted* occupations by any other means than by a *tax* on the tainted, which the tainted are asked to pay so that certain customs and practices not enjoyed by themselves may be passed on? Isn't that the justifaction of aristocracy? That it must be supported out of the wealth created by work it does not participate in so that some value of civilization may be preserved? And your argument about *strength*; you say we need to preserve some older idea of work so that we may have a source of strength to draw on at times when the going is hard; that sounds liks an argument in support of a *warrior class* to me — another aristocratic idea.

WILLIAM: But you are ignoring my main argument.

ARTHUR: That the condition we are in or are entering into is *without precedent* and is full of unusual dangers. But I can show you precedents both in theory and in practice, and from the centuries you profess to admire. First, theory. Let us decline to provide any artificial support to the untainted occupations — to the farmer, the laborer, the craftsman — and let them sink into their natural, underpaid condition, and we arrive at Saint-Simon's Utopia, where ugly work is well rewarded and pleasant work goes cheap. You will argue that his scheme of categories is different from mine: he did not foresee that it would be less demeaning to collect garbage than to edit a newspaper, for instance; but you must expect some change over the centuries — and remember, I am adopting *your* idea of what is desirable and what is ugly.

Second, as to precedent in the actual, I tell you that our situation in this city at this moment is very far from being new. You are obsessed by certain incongruities: there is at present a frenzied interest in fashion and in social position, but, at the same time, families of established position do not take part in public life; the talk is always of beauty, but you see much ugliness; the talk is of exclusiveness, but you see evidence of crowding. And so on. Your metaphor of bodies being inserted into buildings: a steerage, where the talk is of doings among the nobility. Well, you have caught on by now. It is merely *Versailles*, but on a slightly bigger scale; you must allow for larger numbers in everything now. That is a *given*. The palace of the Louis fits all the description you set out. Voltaire tells us it was like a caravanserai, and very uncomfortable. He himself had a room above the privies.

WILLIAM: And where is the King?

ARTHUR: It's a regency. He is a *child*.

William began to look for the young King, which is how he came to know about Sophie Aspair.

She represented the anteroom of what he wanted. Her manner, which was very alert and full of the sense of having received a new infusion of authority (almost as if she had had a transfusion of blood), seemed to say, "I have just seen the King and he looks very well."

Seeing her gave him a chance to put ideas to the test. He

was, as Sophie almost understood as she isolated and humiliated him, a gift to her: someone who took her seriously.

He read that she had given a room of French furniture to a museum and was going to give a big dinner there on the occasion of its first viewing. He found that it was not hard to crash. He observed her. She moved and talked with a nervous energy that she intended to be specific to herself. She understood other aspects of his recent thought, too:

"I'm a Maryland girl, and that's all . . . to it . . . no more!" she said; and for a moment there was evident a small *accent* in her speech.

And she said: "I am most awful . . . can't remember . . . ask *him*. He's the curator!"

William believed that ordinary happiness rose out of what was specific, provincial, and amateur. He believed that Sophie knew this too.

He saw her in an anteroom, or in a series of rooms. The outermost was as crowded as the furniture room of the museum had been when she moved among a throng, slapping and jabbing to show intimacy (and also to move ahead).

In a quieter room she moved more slowly. The jabs were taps on the shoulder. At times her hand lingered. The fine French furniture was along the walls of this room, as he saw it.

And then, by herself. He saw her alone. She stood naked in a large sunlit room. She stretched; she bent. She watched the sunlight on the planks of the floor. After a time she left. The door shut; the latch clicked, and then there was the sound of humans receiving her.

He knew that she was happy in a very ordinary way. William was drawn to this sort of happiness. His pursuit of her futile, however. She firmly intended that everyone alive apart from herself should be abstract, cosmopolitan, and professional.

And wasn't this, in a slightly different way, the intention of the Great Louis?

This was where he was: he had, in a way, found the *court*, and it was very much as his friend Arthur had described it.

He was left on the paths of the city, none of them old enough to suit him.

Where is Tom Guin? he wondered.

EDWARD JONES awakened suddenly. *Lizzie Hannah,* he thought. He got out of his bed and went to a place where he kept old photographs. He looked under *H*; the photographs were filed alphabetically by subject. There he found three photographs: one of Jacob Verdel, Elizabeth Hannah's father; another of Elizabeth Hannah sitting on a lawn with her husband Frederic Hannah; the third showing Elizabeth Hannah with Henry Fourt. Edward Jones looked at this one for some time. Then he put the photographs away in the *H* file, and, for no reason, looked under G. Here he found an old photograph of two men, both smiling broadly. They were both fair-haired and big. How big they were! Edward Jones, a man of modest size, never ceased to be impressed. One man was his grandfather. The other was his grandfather's friend Tom Guin. Each had his arm around the other. They smiled broadly. Around them was an atmosphere of complete happiness. *And yet, at that time they were criminals,* Eddy thought. He looked closely. It never failed to startle him. Both his grandfather and Tom Guin were dressed in clothes that were covered completely with buttons of mother-of-pearl. It never failed to startle him. *Violent dandies,* he thought.

But that's not it, he thought. *It's more than that. It is England and Ireland; they are Irishmen, but the pearl-button idea is cockney; it is high life and low; where they meet in display; and it is friendship. And that, of course, is the important thing.* He put the photograph away.

AT THE HOTEL REX, two old men sat near a window. The window was dirty; it was not possible to see much through it. "Tom Guin was the strongest," one said, speaking low, as though in strictest confidence, "but he wasn't very smart."

10

THE GREENE CLUB

WHEN Edward Jones awakened the following morning, he was still thinking about Lizzie Hannah and Henry Fourt. Tom Guin was not there. Instead there was a new character, Lizzie Hannah's niece, Moo Moo Baker. When Lila Codman called on the telephone, he asked her: "How do you . . . what are the best circumstances under which . . . how does a person see Moo Moo Baker?"

Lila said: "If I knew the answer to that, I'd be the unhappiest girl in New York." Then, seeing that Eddy really did want an answer, she said: "She plays bridge."

Eddy spent the day with cards. He went to a carved box and took out several old decks. He looked carefully at the backs: an Iroquois squaw with a rising sun behind her (he knew she was an Iroquois because it said "Iroquois" quite plainly in gold letters); an English garden; and a spray of gladiolas. He chose the squaw. He held her in his hand. He looked past her. Troublemaker, he thought; he meant Moo Moo Baker, not the squaw.

He pulled a cherry drop-leaf table out into the center of the room and pulled one of the Adam-Sheraton chairs up to it. He sat quite comfortably in the chair; shuffled and dealt the cards: four hands. "Bridge," he said out loud. "Imagine."

When Eddy called up Moo Moo Baker, he said: "Oh, Moo Moo, I'm so glad to find you in. I have a favor to ask. I'm *not* going away this winter and I'm feeling a little impatient with myself for not doing more and I've had the thought that what I'd like best would be to start playing bridge seriously."

"Naturally," Moo Moo said.

Eddy was a little surprised by this response, but he had the presence of mind not to show it.

"And naturally you, Moo Moo," he said, noticing the rhyme, "naturally *you* . . ."

"Are you good?" Moo Moo asked, ruthless.

"Oh *yes*," Eddy said.

"The best people play at the Greene Club. That's where I always play."

"Oh?"

"Are you very good, or just good?" Moo Moo asked.

"Oh, well," Eddy said. "V*ery* good."

And so Eddy found himself, that evening, at the Greene Club. He was not entirely prepared for what he saw. He saw Alice Cuyler, who had pushed (or had not pushed) the head of her young husband Freedy "Kip" Cuyler under water and held it there (or not) until he drowned (he did drown). He saw the Johnny Bassets and the Winthrop Reenys and Van Aspair and several score more of people, all of whom seemed to be on a kind of cruise, the Greene

168

Club being the ship. *Dangerous,* Eddy thought. Then he thought: *one step below charity.* And indeed, as he looked around the room he saw that it was filled with exactly those people whose names used to appear on invitations to charity dances, but no longer did appear there.

Everything looked familiar, but here, familiarity was not a source of comfort. They were in a social hour during which sherry was passed around (not everyone took it; only Van Aspair took more than one; most people sipped sparingly so as not to dull their competitive edge), and it felt like something organized at a school or a spa. And it wasn't just the spirit of organization that seemed familiar; the artifacts were familiar too — the sherry glasses and the tray and the maid, who was, surely, the old crone who used to serve so badly at Mrs. Jimmy Derring's. It was as though he had died and *not* gone to heaven. He was in the wrong place, he felt.

The inmates of the Greene Club had just the opposite opinion. Alice Cuyler gave him a kiss. Sally Reeny waved from across the room and then came almost at a run. And yet in their enthusiasm, Eddy saw with dismay, there was no element of surprise. We knew you'd show up, their manner seemed to say. It was only a question of when.

He was uncomfortable. He was compelled to witness the destruction of one of his favorite ideas: I can go anywhere. It was shown to be prideful. No, no, I can't, Eddy thought. I can't be here. He *was* there, nevertheless.

He found himself in a stagnant calm, a heavy atmosphere that muffled his liveliness. He did not seek to make connections, as he was used to doing. He came across a piece of information and his urge was to leave it where it was. The house, for instance. It was large, neo-Georgian.

He thought: Who built it? He could not help himself thinking this much, but then he stopped. He thought this much and put the rest aside.

He asked no question. He did not ask Winthrop Reeny about his brother Smith Reeny or his sister Mrs. John Clark Kane, or about his mother in Bernardsville, New Jersey (Still ride with the hunt? At her age? Imagine!). He did not ask Van Aspair how Sophie was, and although it occurred to him that Van would know something more than he knew about Victoria Feldman (who had begun to interest him), he did not ask him. Certainly he did not ask Alice Cuyler any question, since any question put to her would come out: *Did you hold his head under water until he was drowned?*

Keep still, he said to himself. *Stand still*. And he did.

After a time, everyone marched out of the room they were in and into a larger room — a ballroom, it must have been — where tables had been set up (perhaps they did not ever come *down*).

The room had the smell of an examination room, which is the smell generated by the mechanical linking of person to person within competitive experience. And it had the hush, the unquiet silence within which schemes in the mind work urgently without talk.

Eddy was thrown off by the silence and the smell. And he was thrown off by the number of people in the room. The room was vast. There seemed to be hundreds of people in it, far more than had been at the social hour. And it was *duplicate bridge*, the same hands dealt around to different partnerships so that everyone would have the same experience by the end. Everything revealed. Perfect justice. No mitigation.

He played almost badly. That is, on those occasions when he played a hand, he did well, but the bidding was confusing to him. Systems he did not know were in force and he imagined — what? That he saw small signals that looked like cheating pass around the table. He had thought (remnant of old assumptions) that Moo Moo would make him her partner for the evening, or that she would see to it that they played together at first so that he might be at ease, but no such thing happened. He saw that his *strategy* — by which he would enter into some attractive activity with Moo Moo (who was an active girl) and seek then (within the benign atmosphere of an attractive activity) to affect Moo Moo's course of action with regard to his friend Henry Fourt — had not only come undone, but had been replaced by another scheme, in which he would find not help for his friend but humiliation for himself. *Serves me right*, he thought.

Just then, seeing with some clarity the limits of what he could expect to achieve by strategy, he found himself breathing air from which all elements apart from *strategy* and *tactics* had been removed. He settled into it.

He found himself, in time, at a table with Moo Moo. He found himself suddenly afraid. He listened. There was a small *crack*. Imperceptible. He played badly. Was there a slight list? He left his cabin and found his friend Henry Fourt in the hall. Henry said that he had heard two officers conversing together and that the ship had apparently hit an iceberg. He and Henry Fourt swore to stick together through thick and thin and went together to A-deck. Men and women were gathered there, some in life preservers (they put them on reluctantly, or with humor, playing down the situation). One man handed up a bit of ice (from the iceberg) and said, "Here, you'd better keep this as a souvenir."

He overbid. He saw Moo Moo and her partner cheat (little hiccups in speech were their signal) and arrive at the perfect bid.

SENATOR SMITH: What did you do then? What was your response?

EDWARD JONES: I overbid.

SENATOR SMITH: What was your purpose?

EDWARD JONES: I didn't want them to get the contract.

SENATOR SMITH: That was all?

EDWARD JONES: That was all.

SENATOR SMITH: What did you do then?

EDWARD JONES: I asked a question and had a thought.

SENATOR SMITH: What was the question? Of whom did you ask it?

EDWARD JONES: The question was: "Moo Moo, is your Aunt Lizzie going to Florida with Henry anytime soon, or will they be in New York for a while?"

SENATOR SMITH: And the question was directed to Moo Moo Baker?

EDWARD JONES: That is correct.

SENATOR SMITH: Did she make a response?

EDWARD JONES: She did.

SENATOR SMITH: Can you tell us what she said?

EDWARD JONES: She said, "Yes, she'll go to Florida, all right, but not with that boring old fairy."

SENATOR SMITH: Those were her exact words?

EDWARD JONES: Those were her exact words.

SENATOR SMITH: Can you describe the situation aboard ship at this time?

EDWARD JONES: We had begun to list quite badly. One lifeboat was ready to be lowered and it seemed to be crowded with men, although there had been a line drawn beyond which only women and children were supposed to go. Van Aspair was in this boat with Mr. Winthrop Reeny and many others whom I did not know, but Mr. Aspair seemed to want to get off.

SENATOR SMITH: Wanted to get off? To give his place to a woman?

EDWARD JONES: No. I do not think that was his reason. He said in my hearing that he didn't want to be in the same boat with a lot of kikes. That was his expression.

SENATOR SMITH: Can you describe your actions as the ship began to list?

EDWARD JONES: Well, as I say, I decided to stick by my friend Henry Fourt. We set off together to see if we could be of any help in launching the lifeboats. Four ladies in particular whom we had got to know well — Miss Brown (her mother was a Miss Mann from Troy, a friend of my mother's); Miss Derwer from Baltimore (her grandmother was a Carroll of Carrollton); Miss Granger from Boston, whom I didn't know, but she was a friend of Miss Brown; and Miss Samantha Young, an acquaintance of Henry Fourt's — we took a particular responsibility for, and we saw them into a lifeboat being lowered off the port side. We worked on more boats on the port side and then the call came: all to starboard, because the ship was listing so badly to port; and we went together to the starboard side and we were quite surprised to see our four friends there. They had not got into the boat after all, or there had been some kind of trouble. Then we heard that there was still room on a boat being lowered on the port side, and we took them there and they did make it safely this time. We returned to starboard and by this time the ship was sinking, and we saw that we must go down with her, but what was terrifying was that suddenly there appeared a mass of humanity — men, women, and children, and we had assumed that the women and children were off. But there was a surge of humanity — men, women, and children, screaming — and up to this point, Senator, there had been no screaming. The water was then right by us. The only thing above us was the hurricane deck or bridge deck, where the funnel came down to the

top. Mr. Fourt and I jumped to try to reach the
deck. We were unsuccessful. Then the wave came
and struck us; the water came and struck us, and
then I rose as I would rise in bathing in the surf,
and I gave a jump with the water, which took me
right onto the hurricane deck, and around that was
an iron railing, and I grabbed that iron railing and
held tight to it; and I looked around and the same
wave that saved me engulfed everybody around me.
I turned to the right and to the left and looked.
Mr. Fourt was not there and I could not see any of
this vast mass of humanity. They had all disappeared. I was taken down with the ship, hanging
on to that railing, but I soon let go. I felt myself
whirled around, swam underwater fearful that the
hot water that came up from the boilers might boil
me up — swam, it seemed to me, with unusual
strength, and succeeded finally in reaching the surface and in getting a good distance away from the
ship.

SENATOR SMITH: How far away?

EDWARD JONES: I could not say, because I could
not see the ship. When I came up to the surface
there was no ship there. The ship would have been
behind me, and all around me was wreckage. I saw
what seemed to be bodies all around. Do you want
me to go through the harrowing details?

SENATOR SMITH: Yes.

EDWARD JONES: The worst was Alice Cuyler. She
was on a raft — some kind of crate, and she was

175

holding the head of her husband under the water and shrieking.

SENATOR SMITH: What was she shrieking?

EDWARD JONES: That she had never liked him, ever.

SENATOR SMITH: And what was Moo Moo Baker doing during this time?

EDWARD JONES: Waiting for me to play from my hand.

SENATOR SMITH: And did you say anything to her?

EDWARD JONES: I did. I said: "Of course, Moo Moo, you're perfectly right. Henry is, from a certain point of view, a boring old fairy, exactly as you say," and then I paused and looked at my hand and then I said, "Of course, someone who had been to Fragattzi's and had seen his work there might have said that he was an *artist*, or at least a good draftsman," and then in rather a matter-of-fact, offhand tone I asked, "Have you been to Fragattzi's recently? They've done it up awfully well, the new man knows his stuff," and then I said, "And someone who had seen him last winter with Lizzie when she was so sick . . ." and I let that trail off.

SENATOR SMITH: Was anything transpiring during the time you delivered this speech?

EDWARD JONES: I was playing spades.

SENATOR SMITH: And did anything else transpire, while you were playing spades. Anything unusual or remarkable?

EDWARD JONES: Yes, Senator.

SENATOR SMITH: Could you describe what happened?

EDWARD JONES: The spirits of the dead surrounded me and tried to comfort me.

SENATOR SMITH: Which spirits exactly?

EDWARD JONES: Kip Cuyler, and Eleanor Brady, who was Van Aspair's first wife and who was bullied awfully by him.

SENATOR SMITH: And did they comfort you?

EDWARD JONES: Oh yes. Kip Cuyler stroked my brow.

SENATOR SMITH: Anything else?

EDWARD JONES: He told me to double-finesse.

SENATOR SMITH: To double-finesse?

EDWARD JONES: Yes. He said Moo Moo had both the king and the jack.

SENATOR SMITH: Did she?

EDWARD JONES: Yes.

SENATOR SMITH: So you made the contract?

EDWARD JONES: Yes.

SENATOR SMITH: Did you make any remark during this time, apart from discussing Henry Fourt?

177

EDWARD JONES: You mean about making the contract?

SENATOR SMITH: Yes.

EDWARD JONES: I just said, "Oh, Moo Moo, did you have both the king *and* the jack? How lucky for us."

SENATOR SMITH: Very restrained. By the way, you mentioned having a thought as well as a question, as all this began. What was the thought?

EDWARD JONES: I thought: *This is very bad form from their point of view.* You see, generally, they don't talk much at these gatherings.

ON THE NEXT MORNING, Eddy discussed with Lila Codman the trouble his friend Henry Fourt was in or was likely to be in.

"I wonder if there is anything *I* could do," Lila asked.

Eddy was silent.

"I could have them to dinner."

"Oh, well."

"You'll help me with that — who the other people should be."

"Oh yes."

They were silent a moment.

"Eddy, imagine Moo Moo pronouncing on Henry's social position."

"Yes, that is awful, isn't it."
"I think Moo Moo's the worst case, don't you?"
"Yes, I think she is."
"Until tomorrow, Eddy."
"Good-bye, Lila."

⸺✦ 11 ✦⸺

THE DUPLICATE

ALICE CUYLER did kill Kip Cuyler. They were out in a boat owned by Harold Goss, who was someone she was seeing.

She was a girl from a small town. She had a heart-shaped face and was *active*. Her father, a high-school principal, was encouraged by the bright look she had and brought her up carefully. She resented this, but kept up her brightness, which she understood to be her asset.

She was happy to marry Kip Cuyler, because he was rich, because he was handsome, and because he was stupid. Because he was stupid, it was easy to convince him of anything. What she wanted to convince him of most was that he had married her because she was pretty.

In time she grew to hate his stupidity. She devised situations that were more and more difficult for him to accept, but he accepted them. Since he believed anything she told him, there was no value intrinsic to his believing that she was pretty. As she held his head under the water, she said: "I don't love you; I never did."

It is hard for people to believe that they have made

180

the right choices. In a certain mood, the happiness of a companion seems to be proof that the wrong choice has been made.

Elizabeth Hannah was like this. The contentment that showed on the face of her friend Henry Fourt seemed to prove that the friendship worked to her disadvantage. She was a thin, grey old woman. She had gone to bed early. She rose up in her bed. It seemed like the dead of night.

Her head was wet like a new baby's. The hair on her head was sparse, like a baby's. Her hair was wet and stringy and lay fastened to her scalp, which was grey and pink. Her eyes turned to the window. *Is he taking advantage of me?* she wondered.

She thought of herself as Roman — the mother of Coriolanus. Her own court was very small: one elderly architect who did not practice. Nevertheless, doubt and suspicion swirled around her, rising, rising, lapping against her toes.

She got up from her bed. She stood straight, as she used to do when she was a young girl attending a convent school. Her body was the body of a wizened child; her head was like that of a new baby. She almost called out: "Sister!"

An unfriendly spirit entered. He was the duplicate of her friend Henry Fourt. He had visited her before. He resembled her friend, but his smile was full of malice.

She leaned forward and spoke to him in a whisper. Secretly, she found the wicked spirit to be exciting.

"You want my money," she said, feeling the excitement of the money.

"What else could it be?" the duplicate replied.

A LIST

EDWARD JONES and Lila Codman drew up a list of people who would be asked to dinner by Lila Codman. It read:

Nicky Parme
Mr. and Mrs. Bobby Prain
Mr. and Mrs. John Hervey
Mr. and Mrs. Pierce Marvell
Lizzie Hannah
Henry Fourt

"That's nine," Lila said.

"You and I make eleven. Sam's not around, I assume."

"Oh no."

"We'll need someone for Nicky Parme."

"Not Sophie. Don't tell me you want Sophie."

"No."

"Thank you."

"What do you think of Victoria Feldman?" Eddy asked.

"Another *Aspair?*"

Eddy laughed.

"Tell me about our party," Lila said.

"Well," said Eddy, "Nicky Parme is good, out of town enough to make it plausible and the name still carries something, and the connection to Sixte is good, a little bit of family; then Bobby and Cintra, good, more family, but then the Herveys and Marvells, quite right, so it isn't just reminiscent and will get around to everyone, and then Lizzie and Henry and the two of us; it will be nice to sit opposite you again, Lila. Eleven is all right. Nicky can just be extra."

"Let's have Victoria Feldman," Lila said.

"Good," Eddy said.

"Eddy, do you want me to wear a lot of jewelry?" Lila asked seriously.

"Oh yes, I think so," Eddy said.

⁂

At the Hotel Rex, a very old man spoke in confidence to two old men who were younger than himself. "There was Timmy O'Neil and Oddy the Jew, and Toomy McDonald and Tilly Rooser and Furly O'Brien and Tarmy DeLaRoy and me. Tarmy and me stuck together. Tarmy came in through Timmy O'Neil; Timmy O'Neil came in through Michael Coonlon. I came in through Tilly Rooser and Tilly Rooser came in with Tom Guin." The old man grew very confidential. "We were all handsome men," he said.

⊸⊷{ 13 }⊶⊷

THE BICYCLE CLUB

SLOWLY, over a period of several days, the form of an old city began to take shape over the newer one. It was felt at the Hotel Rex, where certain old men had trouble in their sleep. Victoria Feldman was aware of *uncertainty*. Edward Jones felt it too. His urge was to *go out*. Nonetheless, he stayed quietly at home. And then, one night, he did go out.

He walked on the streets to a hotel. He felt a small chill, and the wind growing in velocity.

He entered the hotel and went into a large ballroom. He was reminded of the Greene Club. It was a charity event taking place. *Charity*, he thought. And then he thought: *Bridge. All these people will be playing bridge.*

It was an event in honor of a clothes designer. Eddy looked at the clothes. He noticed, especially, the furs. The man, the designer, had a way with fur; it was fur the way the trapper saw it; recently removed from the animal's body.

After a time he thought he would leave, but before he could do so his attention fell on a small, sad man in the seat next to him. Eddy looked at him and then at the other people at the table and then all around the big room; he understood that this man was the designer. Nearly everyone at the table and many other people elsewhere in the room were looking at this man. Some people were waving; some were sending silent kisses and expressions of enthusiasm; but none of these gestures reached the mournful little man — or if they did, they did not warm him.

Eddy saw that the man expected him to say something, but he could not find anything to say. Thinking that it was rude not to say anything, he coughed.

"I am unwell myself," the mournful man said.

"Oh?" said Eddy.

"I live in fear."

Eddy tried to think of what to say next, but he had nothing to say. He coughed again.

"Who do you think designs clothes that are pretty?" the man asked with sudden animation.

Eddy thought. He saw that he must either indicate a very large group of designers (among whom the designer himself would be numbered) or a very small group. He decided on a very small group.

"I think in our time . . . only Balenciaga," he said.

"Exactly," said the little man. He was sadder now than before. Eddy was fascinated by him. The man was in such deep unhappiness that Eddy expected him to cry, but each time a mannequin came down the runway toward him, he watched her with full attention, checking the details of his work.

Once he said: "I use furs just the way they did in your

185

American West," and then he added: "But it is no good, really." Then he said: "Balenciaga. Yes." And then: "All the rest is just making dresses."

Then he got up from the table and Eddy saw him make a slow, mournful progress from table to table, bringing himself to each place, where there was a gesture or a silent kiss waiting for him. He collected these as though they were redundant favors: identical small bottles of scent that he could not quite bear not to gather in. Soon he was laden down with them and looked more sad than ever.

He was waiting at the door when Eddy left. Eddy nodded to him, but the little man ignored this distancing gesture and grabbed Eddy's hand urgently: "You come with me. I have no one to talk to," he said.

Eddy found himself in a darkened limousine. He and the little man were cut off entirely. There was utter silence. The only noise that was perceivable was the sound of the wind against the car.

They entered a huge, dark theater that had been turned into a nightclub. The little man disappeared immediately.

Eddy walked around. He found it interesting. There were quiet places where people stood or sat glumly with no purpose and there were corridors of rapid movement. From time to time, a person who was standing or sitting quietly would enter a stream of rapid movement; sometimes he was carried away quickly; more often he was thrown back by some circular movement within the fast-running current and resumed his former place, more dispirited-looking than before.

Eddy saw one or two well-lit spaces where people seemed to be sitting, not dispirited, but with some sense of their own dignity. Eddy approached one of these areas and found that it was roped off. A man in a dinner jacket guarded the entrance and Eddy did not approach him. Rather, he moved along the rope to a quiet place and looked into the light. There was a sense of calm within the light; men and women moved into it and were interviewed. Eddy watched as a young man took his place in front of the camera.

INTERVIEWER: What are you doing now, Tony?

TONY: I'm working with Prince Alfonso of Savoy.

INTERVIEWER: And what is he doing?

TONY: Swimsuits.

Eddy felt a pull at his sleeve. It was the small designer. "Grotesque," the designer said, meaning Tony and the interviewer. "We can't stay here; it's awful."

Eddy was not sure that he wanted to leave, but the designer pushed him ahead into a rapidly moving stream of people and he was borne along in it. After a while the crowd thinned and the two walked side by side. It was the same as it had been when the designer was looking at his own clothes, Eddy noticed; the little man seemed to be in the deepest unhappiness, but his eyes leaped from place to place as though he were under a terrible obligation to take in every detail.

They were out-of-doors. The night was cold. It came as a surprise: the power of the cold. The designer seemed to feel it too. He saw his car and hurried off to it; but when he noticed that Eddy did not follow, he came back.

"Come on," he said impatiently. "We can't stay here."

"Where will we go?" Eddy asked.

"To a place where they all dress in bicycle clothes,"

the designer said. In his voice was a mixture of excitement, resignation, and disgust. Eddy saw that what was troubling the man was a sense that the visit to this bicycle nightclub *had already taken place.* Eddy was about to say something about this, but the little man interrupted him.

"You're quite right, it will be just nothing; repulsive, really," he said, and then he left abruptly. When he reached his car, he turned toward Eddy and shouted, "Balenciaga!" Then he got into the car and the car pulled away from the curb.

Eddy was alone. He walked down the street a short distance and noticed that he was in a very old part of town. The streets were of cobblestone. He bent down and looked at one. He was quite alone. There was a thin crowd around the entrance to the nightclub, but otherwise the street was empty. He turned a corner and listened. He could hear footsteps. He stood still. A group of men in leather jackets passed by him. He stood still. Another group of men, these dressed in helmets and uniforms of white fabric passed by. (*The Bicycle Club*, Eddy thought). Then there was a small silence, and then more footsteps, growing very loud, finally. Eddy thought: *something old is coming.*

Around the corner came five men. They were very tall. Each had red hair. Eddy looked at what they were wearing. Each one had a suit that was covered in its entirety with buttons of mother-of-pearl. The buttons shone as the men passed beneath the streetlamps.

The five men came up to Eddy. One man stepped forward. He was young, about twenty-five, with red hair and a fair face. He put out his arm and touched Eddy on the shoulder.

"You come away from here now, Mr. Jones," he said.

—⋆{ 14 }⋆—

THE ELECTRIC LIGHT BALL

VICTORIA FELDMAN saw Simon Green almost every night. Usually, he picked her up rather late for dinner, and then, after dinner, they went out. They went to a lot of new places, of course, but they always ended up at the Subway Club, which was a place Simon had a stake in.

Victoria always had a bad time. She didn't like Simon, and she didn't like his friends, and she particularly didn't like the Subway Club, which was filled with people she didn't know. She went out with Simon to avoid disaster (she was sure she was doing the right thing), and then disaster came anyway. She was riding in a taxicab with Simon and Nanno de Huerd (who was the only friend of Simon's she knew herself), and the taxicab pulled up to her door, and she looked up and saw that her apartment had burned down. Not the whole house; just the floor where she lived. Firemen were putting away their things. The second floor was sending out smoke. The windows had been broken. Water dripped down.

"How depressing," Victoria said, thinking, *now I must marry Simon.*

Simon said: "I told you they'd torch you to get you out." (Her apartment was rent-controlled.)

Nanno de Huerd said: "Darling, come to *me*," meaning the Hotel Vaucluse — French scheme of decoration; Château François Premier nightclub; retired whores, courtesans, mistresses, easy ladies, gigolos, pimps, and a few widows, in residence.

So she went to a room at the Hotel Vaucluse, and things were very grim there, with Nanno around all the time and too many drugs (Nanno had a good connection) and too little money — so grim, in fact, that she called up her mother to ask for money, but her mother said no, the lawyers are getting it all (she was proceeding with a suit against Frank Post), and then Victoria asked: *Could I come stay with you?* — meaning in your two rooms at the Hotel Bretagne-Carlton; and her mother said absolutely not, we'd go mad, but she did ask Victoria to lunch at the Bretagne-Carlton, and she did say over lunch that she (Victoria) could charge meals at the B-C (as they always called it), so at least food was taken care of.

Victoria couldn't face going back to her apartment to see what was left, but Nanno said he'd go, and he brought her back a few things (mostly clothes), but he said that nearly everything was charred or waterlogged or both, which was true or not true; and Victoria thought: *maybe he's just selling it all,* but there was nothing she could do about it, so she didn't say anything but "thank you, Nanno, darling"; and he did bring her her mail, which she didn't open right away (she was becoming very lazy), but she did go through it eventually, and in it she found, to her surprise, an invitation to dinner at Lila Codman's. It read:

> *Mr. and Mrs. Samuel Yormin*
> *request the pleasure of your company*
> *at dinner*

and then the date, and the place and the hour. At the very top was the superscription: *To Meet Prince Nicholas de Parme*. It was just a cream-colored card, the kind the stores sell that do sell that sort of thing, but she realized that she hadn't seen one like it in years. Sophie did all her inviting by telephone, and apart from Sophie, Victoria didn't know anybody who gave dinner parties, not really. It made her quite wistful to think how many invitations she used to get. She looked and looked, and thought: *Why me?* — as though she had been a girl from a small mountain village who had received an invitation to the Inaugural Ball in Washington and was in the local papers on account of it — but there was always an explanation for that sort of thing, the girl having written person-to-person to the President, part of a third-grade class exercise on how does our democracy work, singled out for special mention then. This was more of a surprise, and Victoria Feldman was grateful for it and began to plan what she would wear, and then she thought: *At least that's one night I won't have to see Simon.* And then she thought: *What night is it?* Looking, she saw it was that night, four hours away, and she thought: they won't want me now, how awful I am; but she called right away and then (no secretary in between, just an Irish maid) she found that she was talking to Lila Codman.

Something enormous swept over Victoria. The small gods of the apartment, the restaurant, the telephone, folded up. What was with her, soothing, smoothing, lulling, caressing, was something far beyond what those gods knew. She drew confidence from it. In quite an attractive way, she explained about her fire, and she made it sound like an *inconvenience*, like a fire on a steam yacht, in the engine room; *we drifted for hours*, and in fact she did think of one time when the power went out in Frank Post's boat and they did drift in the Gulf of Mexico, which was calm and clear and blue, until someone came to tow them in.

"Of course come," Lila Codman said. "I want to see you."

They gathered at seven forty-five, and were at the table by eight. Lila wore a cream-colored dress in a stiff taffeta. It was the stiffness of cloth that Balenciaga used to use, but it wasn't Balenciaga, of course. The waist was quite high, and the fabric fell away from the waist in a way that implied the Empire. It was very beautiful. What all the world knew, and what no one ever took away from her, was that Lila Codman was well dressed. She had been well dressed as a child, as a young woman, as a bride, as a divorcée, as a bride again, as a divorcée again, as a woman of middle age, as a woman of middle age marrying for the third time, as a woman in the country implying the town, as a woman living tightly, implying ease of movement. Her dress of stiff taffeta implied: the *waltz*; it implied an appearance at court (vanished, possibly, Nicky Parme's or her own); it echoed the cream-white dress she wore on the occasion of her marriage to Henry Codman; it echoed the linen on her bed. It enclosed all the things she had

been and brought them to the surface again for reinter-
pretation in light of new evidence: what she was — an
invalid.

There was no interval between her and the taffeta dress,
although the dress was luxurious and she was now severe.
The dress, like a loyal friend, embraced the new woman
without hesitation, while reminding of the other, healthy
woman, forming then a pivot between what was to be
observed in her now, and what there had been to observe
in the past. Work does not fail a person. A man who has
worked hard with his hands dies with strong hands, and
in the time before his death his hands (loyal friends) do
things for him he could not do for himself. So it was with
Lila and clothes. They rushed to help her. As her spine
shrunk, as her skeleton turned brittle, clothes rose up to
do some of the job, so that she became like an insect who
carries (or wears) his support outside his body.

She was luxurious and severe. Her hair was pulled back
from her forehead. There was no attempt to hide the
pallor of her skin; it was dead white and nearly trans-
parent. There was no color on her or in her except for
jewelry. And here she was humorous — as a little girl is
who puts on adult clothes. Lila, growing light, had put on
heavy jewelry. She wore a necklace of large emeralds and
diamonds, a pin to match (emerald of ten carats), and a
ring (emerald of eight carats). No one had seen these
jewels on her for twenty years.

Lila's guests thought about her jewelry. They thought:
how sick she looks; they thought: how beautiful she is
anyway; they thought: *that dress*; but they came back to:
emeralds. Lizzie Hannah thought: I should have worn
mine. Mrs. Marvell thought: I still have a way to go.

Eddy Jones thought: she is wearing them for me. And

he was right. Reporters did not pester Lila Codman. No one had ever asked her the story about this or that; no one asked her what she thought about this or that or had she done it or not. No one asked her: Who do you dress for? If some person had asked that — Mrs. Yormin, as a member of the Fashion Hall of Fame, tell me, who do you dress for? — she would have answered: I dress for Edward Jones.

She did. She wore taffeta for him, and held her back straight for him, and turned to her right just so for him. The table was for him, and the food, and the talk.

Lila began the talk. She said (as the table sat down): "*Henry Fourt*, I hear that your drawings are the most attractive, the most *sought-after* things in New York City."

"Oh, Lila . . ."

"But it's true. Eddy tells me, *Nina* tells me, every person I meet tells me — every person but you, that is — but I *insist*, because, *if you want to know the truth* — and Nicky, don't be cross — *you* are the guest of honor tonight, because I want to know everything about those drawings."

Lizzie Hannah opened her eyes.

"Well," Henry Fourt said, shy, pleased, eager. "In those days, you know, they put quite a lot of emphasis on *draftsmanship*, which they don't do so much these days, I guess, and they encouraged the more promising students" — and he blushed to be referring to himself in this way — "to think up very large projects. And we did take care, I must say, and we were quite concerned with detail, you see, and of course, we had the most beautiful buildings in Europe to study from." And here, Henry Fourt paused for just a second, but all attention was on him still — Lizzie

Hannah just looked and looked — so he said, "But Lila, you know it's just draftsmanship. That's all it is. It isn't original or important in any way, I'm afraid, and I was very surprised when Fragattzi's said they wanted —"

"*Oh*," Victoria Feldman said. "Do you have something in the show at Fragattzi's?"

Henry Fourt blushed.

Lizzie Hannah looked.

Lila thought: good for you.

Henry Fourt said, "Just one or two drawings."

"*Seven* drawings," Eddy Jones said.

Victoria Feldman thought back. It was not something she was used to doing. She thought back, or *went back*, and saw: line, space, line, and a label. "I saw one," she said, seeing: line, space, line, and a label. " 'Plan for a National Musical Archive.' I think it was the most beautiful thing I ever saw in my life."

"That's one of Henry's," Eddy said.

"He's going to give it to *me*," Lizzie Hannah said, seeing a horrible young girl trying to steal her possession. "It's not for sale."

Lila thought: *well, well, well*, that's enough, and turned to Nicky Parme, and she talked to him in a private voice so that everyone should know that there would not be any general conversation for a while. *Eat quickly, please,* Lila thought, and people did eat quickly. She talked in her low, private voice to Nicky Parme, who was on her right, and then she talked in her low, private voice to her brother Bobby Prain, who was on her left, and it was very much like a family dinner.

Victoria Feldman felt it. She thought: now, she's my

195

cousin, in a way, because she was married to Sixte Aspair, and Nicky Parme is my cousin in a way, because he was a cousin of Sixte Aspair's, and Mr. and Mrs. Prain are Lila's family, so they're in it too, and Eddy Jones must like me, because he bowed to me, and that wonderful man who did the drawings. And *who's that?* she wondered, looking at a portrait of Mrs. James-James Aspair III by Boldini. She didn't know it was Mrs. James-James III, but she knew it was *family*, and she thought: maybe it will be all right after all.

Lila turned from Bobby Prain back to Nicky Parme and talked to him again. Nicky Parme talked in the most attractive way possible about his activities in New York (in the most attractive way possible, he promoted the sale of certain wines and liquors) and about the friends he had seen. Slowly, Lila opened up this talk to include the rest of the table. She asked him questions about certain of the people he had seen, and she said something attractive about each one and said (what she often said) that she wished she could see more of her friends. Then Nicky Parme mentioned a name and Lila did not immediately respond but rather held herself still, thinking: *Here, darling?*

So, Eddy Jones said: "Do you know who I saw the other day? — Moo Moo Baker."

"Oh, *really*," Lila said. "Is she in town?"

"She *lives* in town — why shouldn't she?" Lizzie Hannah said.

Lila put down her knife and fork as though she had just caught herself in the most monumental stupidity. Echo of Sophie. Echo of Mrs. Aspair. Echo of Lila Aspair. Memory of Mrs. James-James II.

"Dear Lizzie," she said. "You see how far things have

gone? I forgot for one minute — if you believe it — that Moo Moo was your — what is she — your niece?"

"I don't see how you could forget that, Lila."

Lila laughed. "First, my mind is going. Second, have pity on me, I don't think of you and Moo Moo in the same breath at all, you see, because while *naturally* you and Henry are about everywhere, I always think of Moo Moo as being more *suburban*."

Lizzie Hannah opened up. Not just her eyes, but her head. Lila felt — what? A certain ruthlessness. She moved away from this, but she could *see* it well enough. Her voice was not ruthless, but standing within her voice she could see: murder, destruction, the uprooting of families for profit, the exclusion of certain ones from the dance floor (echo of the Electric Light Ball), and — victory.

"Which is why I don't think of her as being in *town*," Lila said. She turned to the table. Echo of her father's table in Albany, New York, her father speaking to it: *What did you do today? Account, please.* "Or am I wrong?" Lila asked. "Do people see Moo Moo?"

All lines converged. Sent into the room severally, they hastened to a point. Lila — loop through pleasure, loop through power, small lines sent out to: Sophie, herself when young, herself at present, Mrs. James-James II, Mrs. James-James III (behind her head, wearing pearls, diamonds, ropes of pearls, collars of diamonds) — Lila dropped her voice down to: *command*. "Tell me, I insist," she said. "I get out so seldom. Do people see Moo Moo?"

The table spoke. Nicky Parme said that he was not sure that he actually knew who Moo Moo Baker was; the Prains said no, not for years. The Herveys weren't sure what to say, but Mrs. Marvell, feeling that this was a good time to show that she and Lila Codman had reached an understanding on many subjects, said: "Oh, just *on the court*," at which point Victoria Feldman spoke. She said:

"Oh, Cousin Lila, I know who you mean now. Isn't she the one with the awful skin?"

Lila looked. *That's enough now,* she thought. Aloud she said (after a small laugh), "I'm afraid none of us can expect to have your good skin, Victoria." She looked over at Lizzie. *Don't rile her now,* Lila thought. She made her voice more gentle. "Lizzie dear, I didn't mean to be hard on Moo Moo. I know she has her good points; it's just that I think of you and Henry as being two of the most cosmopolitan people I know, and I just don't think of Moo Moo that way."

Lizzie Hannah's mind, open for a time, closed up again. It swallowed the word *cosmopolitan* and shut up. That was it. She and Henry Fourt were cosmopolitan. It was as clear as day. She and Henry were cosmopolitan and if Moo Moo didn't understand, it was because she wasn't cosmopolitan.

"But if she's in town so much, I ought to see her," Lila went on, gentle, smooth, *all right now? Baby ready for bed?*

Lizzie, big baby, all smoothed out, said:

"Actually, she spends most of her time in Greenwich."

Eddy looked at Lila, and he thought: I must get her to bed now, she is so tired. He looked up. Dessert came at best speed. Talk continued, not general, two or three small conversations. *Get her to bed,* Eddy thought.

Eddy said, "We'll have coffee in the library," in a way that said: those who insist on coffee may take it in the library, and Lila said nothing, but got up and then wavered a bit. She stood at the head of the table and was a little unsteady, which the table noticed. The table turned to Eddy and saw that what his face said was: *go home.* And they went. Nicky Parme spoke softly to Lila and went. The Prains spoke softly and went, and so did Victoria Feldman. The Herveys and the Marvells would have liked to stay, but they found no support for this idea, not anywhere, so they left. Lila didn't give them much of a good-bye at all, just a small smile. Lizzie, oblivious, continued at her own pace, so that she and Henry Fourt were the last to go. Lila disappeared. Eddy saw them to the door. Eddy thought: More or not? Eddy thought: *nail it down.* He spoke in a confidential tone of voice. He said: "Henry, I have a favor to ask. She's very sick, as you see. If you're going to be here this winter, I hope you'll spend some time with her."

Lizzie looked at him. "What?" she asked.

"Lila is so fond of Henry," Eddy said. "I hope that if he is going to be here this winter he will call on her often."

"Well, he's *not* going to be here this winter," Lizzie said. "We're going to Florida right away." And then she said what was not the truth, since, in fact, she had felt, during dinner, a rise of health and of spirits. She said: "*Right* away, because I haven't been feeling well myself."

Eddy saw them out to the elevator, but did not wait for the elevator to come. He closed the door on them. Then the door opened, and Henry came back in. He spoke quickly (*must not keep her waiting,* he was thinking).

"Don't mind Lizzie's selfishness," he said.

"Oh *no,*" Eddy said.

"You know we're terribly happy together."

"I *know,*" Eddy said.

"At least *I'm* terribly happy. I've never been so happy in my life."

"Good," Eddy said.

"Good night, Eddy," Henry said.

"Good night, Henry," Eddy said.

Lila was in the library, waiting for just one sentence or two with Eddy, remainder of that habit: first word in morning, last word at night.

"Oh, darling, did it go?" Lila asked.

"Oh *yes*."

"I'm so glad."

"Thank you."

"Oh . . ."

A rhythm beat out from Lila. There was nothing to interrupt it. It was a good, steady beat. It said: any-time, any-time, any-time. And then: any-thing, anytime, any-thing, anytime. Lila got up.

"Victoria Feldman came after all," Eddy said.

"Oh yes. She had a fire at her house. She told me all about it. She's stopping at the Vaucluse."

"The V*aucluse?*"

"The Vaucluse."

"Imagine."

"Imagine."

Ellen, Lila Codman's old maid, was standing in the doorway, not shy to overhear. She took Lila by the arm.

"Good night, darling," Lila said.

"Good night, Lila."

Eddy, shy, said to Ellen, "You might tell Mrs. Yormin how we think she looks."

"Oh," said Ellen. "There's no one looks like Mrs. Yormin. Not ever."

"That's just what we do think," Eddy said. "Ellen and I."

Lila looked at him and left. The rhythm beat into the room and left. Eddy was left alone. The best room in New York, he thought. He sat in it.

·••≼ 15 ⊁••·

IN THE OLD CITY

LLEN came into the room. She took away the
coffee tray and then she returned. She just stood.
Eddy said:

"How are you, Ellen."

"Fine and dandy, Mr. Jones."

Eddy felt the reversal: Master Edward Jones standing
before Mr. Robert Prain. *Ask me then,* Eddy thought.

"Mr. Jones," Ellen said. "I wonder do you read the
papers?"

"Oh yes, Ellen," Eddy said.

"I wonder, do you ever see the *Poll*?"

"Yes," Eddy said. He did. He read every paper every
day.

"Do you know the part they call 'Miss Quality'?"

"I know it, certainly."

"Well, I want to ask you something, Mr. Jones. When
I was a girl in New York — and I know you know about
New York, Mr. Jones — we used to have gangs. Evening

would come and my mother would say, 'Pull down the blinds, Ellen, the gangs are out.' "

"Yes."

"And that wasn't all. My cousins were in them, and my father, maybe he was too."

"Yes?"

"My father was in them."

Eddy opened his eyes a little wider. He felt the small effort in his forehead and all around his eyes. He waited.

"My father was what you call a Dead Rabbit, Mr. Jones. He was in what you call the Dead Rabbits. What I want to know, Mr. Jones, is, in the papers they have them again, the Rabbits. *Have they been going all this time?*"

Eddy looked at Ellen. He was aware of his own person: his arms and legs, his fingers and hands. He was aware of his clothes: the dinner suit, his grosgrain tie, his patent-leather shoes (the only shoes he could buy in a store), his black silk stockings, his gold studs, and his cuff links — buttons of mother-of-pearl one button gift of Michael Coonlon, Pearl Button Gang, jumped up out of it, the other three matched to it by Jassern Gress, jeweler, third floor, six East Fifty-seventh Street; button linked to button by platinum, one button on each link made small by Gress to fit easily through a buttonhole.

"No, not exactly," Eddy said, feeling the links, button to button, Troy to Albany, Protestant to Roman Catholic. "But there might be a connection."

Ellen stood, quiet. Her hair was white, but not dead white — shiny white. Her eyes were blue.

Eddy looked at her. "You don't have to be afraid," he said.

"Oh no," Ellen said. "Not me or you either. But some of them should be."

Eddy didn't answer and she left. After a minute, he went out into the night.

To the new city the old one came as wind. It blew along the streets and sent people inside.

Victoria Feldman felt the wind as she entered the Hotel Vaucluse. Everything felt older. She felt old and powerful. She put her hand to her neck. *My neck is long and graceful*, she thought.

She stood within a small elevator. *La Belle Mlle. Aspair au long cou*, she thought. *Where did I get that from?*

The descending shape brought an answer:

Your mother's aunt, Cornelia Aspair, was the most beautiful girl of her day. She was presented at Berlin and at the Court of Saint James. The French called her *La Belle Mlle. Aspair au long cou*. Her mother was the woman in the portrait.

"Mrs. James-James Three," she said aloud. Usually she was so vague about the family; suddenly she was not vague. She was quite definite. She saw it all in her mind; not just the genealogy of the family (it came to her in every ramification), but the complicated history of the succession *within* the family. She saw Johannes I give way in a natural way to Johannes II, but then, she observed, the succession was not to any son but to *Mrs.* James-James II, and then to *Mrs.* James-James III (the woman in the portrait), and *then what?* She saw that the elevator was quite dirty. "Well, then through Sixte, because he still had money, and that's how it gets to Sophie," she said.

Suddenly she was quite depressed. She was at her floor

and she didn't see any way that anything was going to get from Sophie to her. "Still," she said, "I don't see why I have to marry Simon Green if Lila Codman is going to take me up." She stood in the dark hallway. The hallway was decorated with painted wooden panels. It was supposed to be lighthearted and French. Everything at the Hotel Vaucluse was supposed to be that way. Most of her confidence had gone, but a small amount remained. "I won't marry Simon," she said. "He doesn't even know I have a pretty neck."

The old city lowered itself onto the newer one. Men came into the streets who wore the bloody pelts of dead animals pinned to their shirts; also men who wore bowler hats at a rakish angle as though to say, "See how we like the sport"; also redheaded men, shining like noon, cruel-looking, covered from head to toe with buttons of mother-of-pearl.

Ellen, alone in her small room, having put Lila Codman safely to bed, felt the old city come onto the new. "Pull down the blinds, Ellen, the gangs are out," she said to herself.

On the street, the Pearl Button Gang formed around Edward Jones. They led him onto an old path that was like a trench.

Eddy, with the Pearl Button Gang around him, came up to a man who was about to strike down another man with a knife.

Eddy said, "No, don't do that."

The man with the knife heard the sound of a voice and

turned toward it. He saw five tall, redheaded men, shining like noon, cruel-looking, covered from head to toe with buttons of mother-of-pearl. He fled.

Edward Jones, a small man in evening clothes stood in a street in New York City. A man with a knife ran away from him in fear.

"No one will ever lay a hand on you," Eddy said under his breath, meaning the young man he had saved from attack.

The old city moved into the new one and mingled with it. At the Hotel Vaucluse, Victoria Feldman pulled down the shades of her window against the night. At Lila Codman's it occurred to Ellen to check to see if her mistress was all right. At the Hotel Rex, a very old man felt the city of his youth rise all around him. He saw a friend. "There's Tarmy!" he said.

Sophie Aspair was at home. She was not alone. In fact she was surrounded by company. Dinner was over; the President of the United States was making his way to the drawing room, where he would, inevitably, sit in the small barrel-backed chair standing away from the wall.

Suddenly Sophie felt the old city. She had never felt it before. She felt it as panic and then, forgetfulness. *Who are these people?* she wondered, looking at a room full of strangers.

✄

"WILLIAM GUIN," the young man said, introducing himself.

Hearing "Guin," Edward Jones said:

So Tom Guin says to me: "Here's what we'll do. Tammany's going to lay it on, we'll lay it on bigger. They make a big play, see, bucket of coal and a chicken. A lick and a promise. We'll make them look like pikers."

Then he turned to the young man and said (simply, as though they had been talking together for some time), "Tom Guin went up against Tammany, you know."

"Oh, I know," William Guin said, "and got beat."

They walked together for quite a long time, in a very friendly way. Eddy told as many stories as he could remember about Tom Guin (all of which he had heard from his grandfather); William Guin told Eddy his theories about work. Eddy was surprised to hear that he had been to Sophie Aspair's.

"That would be the *court*, you see," William Guin said.

"There might be *other places*," Eddy said.

It occurred to Eddy that there was material enough for another conversation on another day, and so, taking the initiative, he said, "I hope you will come to visit me at the place where I live."

William Guin said that he would. They exchanged practical information and it seemed for a minute that they would part, but they both felt it was *too soon*, so they went on. Eddy pointed out one or two old paths William Guin might want to take. William Guin said:

"You do see what I mean about work."

"Oh yes."

"Men don't get to know each other in any other way."

"Yes."

"Men will work for almost no money simply to be in the

company of other men. If a man wants to say a gentle thing to another man, the easiest way is to praise the other man's work."

"The best way to be affectionate with a woman is to say you like what she has on."

"Common sense."

"Common sense."

"Without it?"

"Calamity."

They parted. Eddy stood alone, feeling cold. Then the five red-haired men came up to him at a run and, running, grabbed him. He ran, carried along by them.

To his left and right he saw an enormous crowd of killers and thugs; gangs of killers and gangs of thugs. There were Dead Rabbits and River Rats and Bowery Boys and Plug Uglies. A man with one tooth bit a young girl and took away her ear.

PLUG UGLY: I did it with me gums!

ANOTHER: Ah, ya still have one tooth left.

Eddy was carried along safely by the five red-haired men. He thought:

There were ten thousand men, women, and children out on the racket, all paid for by Tom Guin. Oh, Lord, wasn't it a show. We lashed three barges together, and we had two steamboats pulling them and two tugs besides. There were so many people, we couldn't land at Yonkers the way it was planned, but what did we need to land at Yonkers for, the time we were having right there on board. A thousand kegs of beer: Eagle, Toler, Hammer's; a ton of oysters; hams, chickens, turkeys, bread puddings, suet puddings — all so much you couldn't eat it. And then stealing it, putting it in your pocket, the old women shoving it down in their bosoms, or up under their skirts. Wasn't that a laugh, when Tom didn't care, as it was all for them. "What do I care?" he said. "If they steal it it's because they need it." And then the ice cream, no way to steal that easy, the day being hot, and no way to stick it next to the bosom, so then they hollered in complaint:

"I saw one got four plates and I only got three."

Tom Guin said, "We'll get you a fourth," and he did. "Don't forget to tell your husband to vote for Tom Guin on election day," he said, handing it over.

And the songs. I remember we used to sing "My Old Straw Hat," I think we sang that, and "Little Freddy," that was a sad song, and "Over the Sea."

> My old straw hat
> Have you seen, have you seen
> My old straw hat.
> It's been out on the sidewalk
> It's been up on the stair
> Now I can't find it anywhere
> My old straw hat.

They were in an enormous crowd. The five red-haired men pushed Eddy forward through it. He saw that they were on a pier. They came to the end and the six of them leaped across from the end of the pier to the lashed-together barges as the barges pulled away. The five men all patted Eddy on the back as if to say that he had done very well, and the leader bent down to straighten his clothes.

RED-HAIRED MAN: Dressed like a gentleman.

The red-haired men withdrew. They left Eddy in a fine place, from which he was able to see: everything; all the fine women and men; the dancing; the happiness. Eddy was beside himself and he very nearly cried out, but he stayed still.

He could not control his wish to be closer to the dancing, however. Step by step, he moved closer. It was a two-step they were dancing to, or a waltz. He could not tell. He was pierced by it. He came closer to it. At every step he took, some of the dancers fell away. Finally, there were only two: his own handsome grandfather and a fair, round woman. *I didn't know she was so plump,* Eddy thought. Then his grandfather stepped back and he was left alone with his grandmother.

The world was curved. Its surface was like a curved piece of glass with light under it. She smiled. Then she moved her lips. He moved closer to hear her. What she said was: "Lila."

He went into Lila's room. A doctor was there, and Samuel Yormin. They both left.

"Oh, Eddy," Lila said.

Eddy got into her bed and arranged her so that her head was on his shoulder, as it had been before at other times, at football games and boat races. At football games and boat races, Lila Prain, meant to be in the company of some athlete, kept *that* young man at a distance, but came up to

Edward Jones (matter of habit, matter of trust) and put her head on *his* shoulder, as she had again done at her wedding to Henry Codman, giving Edward Jones the second dance (after Codman), putting her head gently on his shoulder as they went around in front of the whole room (not having done this for Codman), and then again when her son Edward Codman had had his first trouble and his second.

Eddy told her all his best stories, all the ones she knew, and she said "yes, yes" from time to time; and then he told the ones he had held for last — how Mary Carmody had said: *Do you want a brewery, Michael?*; and how they had come up the river to Albany, taking the Erie Shandaken; and how his grandfather had said: *And I have been a rich man ever since.* Then he told her about his grandfather dying, they so close, and how it was with old Sam Koerner, and the man who gave him the silver dollar, and all the flowers.

Lila said: "Like that, please, Eddy. Lots of flowers. No little plain-clothes thing. In town, Eddy, at a big church, *packed to the rafters.*"

"Oh yes," Eddy said.

"Flowers like your grandpa had, *and the bishop.*"

Then she grew very tired and began to drift. He held her and put his right hand to her forehead to hold her in herself. He told her the last, best story — how, turning from flowers, he saw: a pretty girl. He said: how she was dressed, how she held herself — quite like a girl, but in a way few women ever know — and how she seemed to rise up out of Coonlon and Jones and flowers; and how (again) she was dressed: white shift, loose waist, hanging just so.

Lila, drifting, saw her and said: "Oh, Eddy, she sounds perfectly lovely."

Eddy said, "But of course, Lila, it was *you*." And he thought: just think how lucky we have been; but he knew this to be an afterthought just for himself. He held her for a moment, then looking, saw a bubble formed on her lips, *last air*. It was not attractive and he burst it. Take inventory, he thought, and he left her. He went into the next room, where the doctor and Samuel Yormin were, and he thought: *none of these men know anything about women.* Out loud he said: "She ought to be *laid out*. I'll choose the clothes." He left. He went into the street.

He walked about for a bit, quite calm. He passed the Bretagne-Carlton, where Biki Post was asleep (two Diunal before retiring), and the Hotel Vaucluse, where Victoria Feldman was restless in sleep. Thinking of Victoria Feldman, Eddy thought: *good luck to you.* He went into his house and sat (familiar spot) in the last grey of the morning.

At the Hotel Rex, an old man stood in the middle of a circle of old men. "He's dead," the man in the middle of the circle said. The men in the circle opened their eyes a little wider. They thought back, remembering the tiny old man who had shrunk and died. They thought of his tiny arms and his tiny shrunken head. "He was a very fierce man," the man in the middle said. "He was in with the Pearl Button Gang."

The old men moved around and around in a circle. After a time they stopped. They exchanged pieces of clothing. Now, one man wore the shirt of another.

ONE MAN: Keep the Devil off your back.

Then in a dormitory room smelling of urine and liquor and sweat, with a small, sweet death-smell too, each one went to his bed.

At the Hotel Vaucluse, Victoria Feldman rose out of a restless dream. "Look," she said. "The old men are sleeping."